NUMBERS ASCENDING

REBECCA RODE

ONE
LEGACY

As ALWAYS, the Firebrand pretended not to notice me. He stood at the corner, arms crossed, expression amused, as he watched the army of excited schoolmates navigate the hallway. The same gray T-shirt he'd worn most of the school year pulled tight around his shoulders, coming to a V where he'd left it unbuttoned to expose his collarbone. It was that and those startling gray-blue eyes that melted most girls' hearts.

Most—but not all. I was one of the few who knew what he was, which meant staying far away. Our interactions were limited to a simple walk-by after school.

His eyes skipped over me. It would have been convincing had his shoulders not tensed as I passed.

Me: Eighty-two.

Firebrand: Zero.

There wouldn't be an eighty-three. With it being the last day of school, the hallway was packed with chattering graduates moving more slowly than usual, calling their goodbyes and promising to stay in touch. As if any of them would still be friends a year from now. After our Declarations tomorrow, most would be traveling to the new lives they'd chosen and their permanent homes.

Except me. My life had been chosen for me before I was born. Maybe even before my parents were born. Gram, or Her Honorable Treena Hawking, as people called her, had given the country every shred of freedom they'd asked for—retiring the Rating system and moving everyone to the coast. Letting them choose how they spent their lives.

Unless they were her posterity. Then we were cemented into politics as tightly as the metal statue of Gram was cemented in front of the Block.

I looked over my shoulder at the crowded hallway one last time, fixing it in my memory. My actual memory, not my implant files. The sickly blue walls surrounding me, covered in colorful wall-ad screens. The gray tile floors. The heavy body odor that never left despite the contingent of janitors who attacked the campus each night. Just a building full of classrooms housing a thousand memories. I had fought so hard to come here, to ditch the professor who'd tutored my twin brother Alex and me, begging my parents for the opportunity to be normal.

Normal. The very idea was laughable. Three years at a public school did not a normal teenager make. My ex-boyfriend, Derik, was proof enough of that.

The Firebrand was watching me.

I slowed, meeting his gaze with a challenge of my own. He jerked and tore his eyes away, fixing his attention on a wall screen that read *Congratulations, Graduates*! At least the school had taken a break from its relentless "fundraising" ads to offer us a useful message.

Firebrands, the fringe political group that wanted Dad removed from office, didn't talk to Hawkings. Not even on the last day of school. And Hawkings most definitely did *not* interact with Firebrands. It was one of those laws both sides simply understood.

A professor walked by and nodded to me, unable to hide the relief on her face. Another graduating class gone. Another year finished. The Hawking heiress swept off to her fake future in politics and out of her hair forever.

Only one professor had ever felt comfortable in my presence. And, as luck would have it, they'd fired her halfway through the year for having a frank conversation with me about my not-so-stellar grades. She had been right, but that didn't matter. One message from His Honor Dad Hawking and the school had withdrawn like a snail in the afternoon sun. The message was clear: leave Legacy Hawking alone.

They had. *Everyone* had. I felt like the brightly colored fish at Dad's office, alone and cursed forever in a luxurious aquarium.

The crowd slowed as we neared the doors, and I groaned. The door tradition. Each year, the school's staff stood outside and clapped for those stepping through the doorway into adulthood or some such nonsense. That was fine, but the students also felt it necessary to pose, hovering over that stupid threshold in a silly way while their friends took captures.

Easing to the right, I squeezed through a gap between two bodies, getting an irritated "Hey!" from one girl. The expression that came to her face when she recognized me was hilarious. What was I going to do, arrest her? I didn't have the power to repaint my own bedroom. Not when the tabloids analyzed every color, texture, and fabric. Designers from all over the country had competed on a national broadcast for the opportunity of their lives. Not one had asked for my opinion.

The side door came into sight. I finally squeezed myself free, imagining a sucking sound as I did, and shoved the door open. The fresh air felt like a cold shower on a hot day. The sidewalk was nearly as crowded as the hallway, and transports packed the street, but not a single person looked at me. Not the students, not the professors, not the guards. For the first time in months, I felt completely free.

It lasted half a second. A message arrived from my driver, Travers. It floated in my vision beneath the digital time, the words blurring the background beyond them. YOU'RE LATE. WHERE ARE YOU?

I blinked, sweeping the implant message away without a response, but my euphoria had already begun to deflate. The moment was gone.

The door opened behind me. "You going to block the door all day?"

I turned to find Firebrand Guy staring down at me, his eyes widening in recognition. This was the closest we'd ever stood. The air around him smelled faintly of day-old musk and sea salt. He wore his black hair spiked messily in a very I-don't-care way that gave him the illusion of even more height than he had. His eye color perfectly matched the clouds overhead.

It wasn't his eye color that startled me. It was the depth in them, the lifetime of pain they carried.

I cleared my throat, breaking eye contact. Apparently our silent pact was over, but that didn't mean I'd won. "I might. I like this doorway."

"Your father may own the country and every other door in the building, but you can't have this one. It's how I've escaped every day this year." Now his eyes glinted with silent laughter.

A smile threatened, but I wrestled it into submission.

"I'm afraid your secret has been discovered. Although neither of us will be using it again with Declarations tomorrow."

"Lucky us. We get to move from one prison to another. I'm Kole."

"Legacy."

"Yeah, I think I knew that." He adjusted his shirt. I didn't mean to follow the movement, but my eyes locked on the exposed collarbone before I remembered. Firebrands didn't get their tattoos until they turned eighteen. This guy wouldn't have taken the oath yet.

It didn't make him any less dangerous.

His eyes hardened as he followed my gaze. "You shouldn't be out here alone. Don't you usually have an army following you around?"

"Nah. That's my fan club." A second message from Travers arrived. I dismissed it without reading it. "I do have an impatient driver, though. He'll be here any second."

"A driver. Of course."

I folded my arms. "Let me guess. You take the train home with your Firebrand buddies and discuss how oppressed you are under my dad's rule. You cry the entire trip and take a whip to your back when you get home."

"Not true. I walk home." His mouth twitched. I wasn't the only one struggling to keep a straight face. "See you tomorrow, princess. Or do you even have to Declare when the entire country knows about your sweet gig at Daddy's office?"

"A position I earned as much as anybody."

"By what, failing your classes and scowling at the world? Three-quarters of the school is more qualified, so spare me the excuses."

I tamped down my immediate reaction, which was to

send a fist through his too-perfect nose. "You have no idea what my life is like."

"And your dad has no idea about mine. Which is a problem, don't you think?"

"He could help your little group if you'd stop demanding impossibilities."

"Restoring the Rating system isn't an impossibility. It's an inevitability." He leaned closer, his gray eyes capturing my attention once more. "And the Firebrands are anything but a little group."

Then he was striding down the sidewalk in the direction of the Shadows.

Typical Firebrand activist—smug, overconfident, and whiny. I cursed, angry at myself for letting him have the last word. Firebrand: One.

I watched his tall figure stalk down the sidewalk until he disappeared around a corner. The guy really was walking home. Because he couldn't afford the train fare or because he was too stubborn to follow the crowd? Something told me it was the latter.

And he was wrong about the Rating system. Anybody who meant to cure our country's problems by slapping numbers on our heads to control us had a screw loose somewhere.

A clean matte-black transport slowed and pulled to the side of the six-lane street in front of me, looking out of place next to the ad-plastered models in traffic. Travers leaped out, all lean and lanky angles in his black uniform, the light catching what little gray hair he'd managed to keep. He yanked the door open for me—a formality considering the door could open on its own.

"Given your expression," he said, "I'll forgo asking how

your day was and remind you that the tutor is waiting at home."

I climbed in and plopped onto my usual seat. The butter-soft white plastic curved to my body after years of use. The harness swung down automatically and fastened itself around me with a click. "My expression is the same as normal."

"You look ready to murder someone. So, yes, a normal day at school." Travers shot me a pointed look as he closed my door and climbed into the front right seat.

Of all my father's employees, Travers was my favorite. He could be insistent at times and a little obnoxious about my schedule, which Dad liked, but he knew when I needed a distraction from the heaviness and drama of life in the spotlight. He also taught me odd things like transport maintenance. On a rainy day a few years ago, he'd shown me a secret access code that unlocked all transport doors. I still remembered it. I always tipped him despite Dad's insistence that his salary was high enough.

"I ran into a Firebrand," I muttered.

"Home, please," Travers called out. The vehicle clicked a confirmation and moved smoothly back into traffic. Then he looked over his shoulder. "Ah. That sounds painful."

I rolled my eyes. "Technically, he ran into me. Or almost did." I was rambling now. "At first I thought he was quieter than the others and less obnoxious, but I was wrong."

"Quiet means dangerous. Never know what they're planning in those scheming heads of theirs. I'm glad you know better than to fraternize with such people. They threaten everything your grandmother has sacrificed so much to establish." Travers shook his head and faced the front again. "Now, back to your schedule for today. The tutor awaits for your final run-through of tomorrow's Declaration, then the hairdresser arrives to touch up your color. Your father should be home for dinner. I'm told he plans to give you and your brother a pep talk of some kind. Then—"

"I'm not going home yet. I want to see Gram."

He stiffened. "I'm sure your grandmother can wait until tomorrow."

"Professor Vine had several decades left in him last I checked. Gram doesn't."

The joke passed right over him. "The Honorable Treena Hawking sleeps in the afternoons. Meanwhile, Professor Vine can't polish your Declaration without you."

"Sure he can. He wrote it in the first place."

"Perhaps we could have made a stop if you'd been on time, but we're already a quarter of an hour late."

"I had to say goodbye to some friends. Graduation is a big deal. Or don't you remember? I know it was a long time ago for you."

"All those friends. I'm sure that took awhile."

I stared at my hands. "Sure did."

The smile left his eyes. "I know you resent your father's lectures about the importance of tomorrow's announcement, but I agree with him this time. The entire country will be watching you. That's a privilege to be taken seriously."

I cringed at the word "privilege." It was too often used as a weapon against me. "I already know how to say, 'I'm following in my father's honorable footsteps and doing exactly what every Hawking ever has done. Yes, I'm irrelevant, and no, I don't care. Thanks for the tax money and my big house'."

Travers sighed heavily. "At least you acknowledge

where your father's money comes from, which is more than most politicians accomplish in a lifetime."

"I'm a quick learner. Transport, course correction. Take us to Gram's house." The transport clicked in affirmation and veered right, out of traffic and toward the clearer sky of the coast. The tall buildings towering over the road immediately grew less frequent. The closer we got to the coast, the less there was of anything—except weeds and tangled forestland. Experts said it was due to some tsunami a century before, but Gram had other theories.

Travers moaned. "You were so much easier as a young child."

I grinned. "Don't worry, I'll be quick."

"Quick? Which version of quick will this be, Miss Hawking? Your speed at which you left school today, or the speed at which you got ready for school this morning and every other day this year? Or perhaps your last visit to Gram's house, which lasted four hours when you asked for ten minutes?"

"Quick *enough*. You don't need to . . ." I trailed off as a message scrolled across my implant screen, floating in my vision.

MESSAGE RECEIVED: DIRECTOR VIRGIL, NEUROMEN LABS
GREETINGS, MISS HAWKING. WE WISH TO OFFER YOU THE POSITION OF LAB SPECIALIST AT NEUROMEN LABS.
WE HOPE YOU CHOOSE TO ACCEPT THIS HONOR AT YOUR DECLARATION TOMORROW.
IT WOULD BE A PLEASURE TO ADD A HAWKING TO OUR PRESTIGIOUS PROGRAM ONCE AGAIN.

I felt my hands curl into fists. Neuromen had created our brain implants and software, although Gram insisted the technology had been around for decades. But most importantly, it was also the lab where Mom had worked, where she'd invested her entire soul and over twenty years of back-breaking work.

The place she'd died.

How dare Director Virgil send me this after what happened to Mom? Did he live in some delusion that I would actually appreciate the gesture? The message may as well have said, "Thanks for sacrificing your mom. Who's next?"

"Miss Hawking?"

The transport was unbearably hot despite the spring chill. If only I'd worn my short-sleeved dress instead of the more sophisticated gray wool one. I dismissed the message and shot Travers a tight smile. "Yep?"

Travers gave me a long look. "We're arriving now."

We pulled up the circular driveway in front of Gram's coastal home with its newly painted light-purple exterior. Gram's pick. It matched the stone necklace she'd worn since before Dad was born. The structure stood two stories tall and was oddly narrow. Gram could have chosen any of the long-abandoned mansions in town, but she'd insisted her frail body ran on salt and sea wind and she didn't mind how old and run-down it was.

Travers climbed out and held the door for me. I blinked a few times, transferring a tip via the IM-NET, the invisible web that connected our implants. He accepted it with a barely perceptible nod.

"This may be a good time to finish that book you've been hiding under the seat," I told him as I slid out, lifting my dress to avoid the mud. "The one with that busty blonde on the cover. Or was it a brunette this time?"

"Blonde, and I finished it yesterday," he said quickly, his eyes flicking to the guards pulling the door open for me, fists to their chests. By law, old-fashioned paper books belonged in protected museum environments. Not that any museum would want this kind. Its cover was delightfully scandalous.

"I'll see if I can find you another, then. Can't have you sitting out here bored all the time." I winked. His mouth twitched, but he kept his composure for the guards' sake. Then I strode into the darkness of Gram's manor.

TWO
KOLE

BESIDES MY MORNING RUN, the forty-minute walk home from school was usually the most pleasant part of my day. Dirty and unkempt as the sidewalks were the closer I got to home, they held fewer ad boards than the main part of town. And since few in the Shadows could afford transports, the roads lay wide and quiet beside the occasional train zooming past. I still had to endure the tiny ads moving across the bottom of my vision as, unfortunately, I wasn't likely to afford their removal anytime soon. But after the crowded halls of school, any peace made the walk worth it.

Today was different. My mind kept wandering back to forbidden areas, like Legacy Hawking. No matter how I tried to distract myself, she'd worm her way into my thoughts like an annoying advertisement.

The first problem was that Uncle Dane knew she attended my school. He'd discovered it last year and had drawn up all kinds of plans for me to take advantage of the situation—spying on her, a false friendship, even a fake romance. He'd tried to convince me of its importance to the cause. The word "duty" had come up at least a dozen times.

In the end, my one protection was the fact that I didn't know her and she had no desire to know me. And I intended to keep it that way. It was safer for both of us.

But today I'd been weak. With school finally over and some semblance of freedom within my grasp, I'd been sloppy about my retreat. Legacy Hawking wasn't supposed to know I existed, and the Hawkings were supposed to ignore us as they always did.

A simple conversation, nothing more.

That brought me to the second problem. Legacy Hawking wasn't a girl you could easily forget. She was stunning. Not beautiful like the made-up and overcorrected models on IM-NET ads but truly and naturally stunning. Her eyes glowed a true green, no dyed implant lenses required. While her twin brother dressed with a focus on trends, Legacy's style seemed more understated and timeless. Where her brother embraced every chance to appear on camera, Legacy shunned attention and crowds. Rumor had it she'd chosen to attend our school against her parents' wishes. I wasn't convinced. It would make her the first Hawking in generations to descend to our level, and I couldn't figure out why any celebrity would want that. The idea intrigued me.

I'd convinced myself for three years that I didn't care. Now I had to remind myself all over again.

I crossed the street against traffic, dodging a battered transport sporting a clothing ad, and pulled up the warehouse invitation in my implant files. The management position was truly mine. Even better, it lay 156 kilometers away. Too far to fulfill my uncle's demands yet close enough to visit Mom in the hospital on weekends. When I had enough saved up, I'd have her moved closer to me. We would finally escape my uncle's influence and my dad's shadow once and for all.

It was also far enough away I would never have to think about Legacy Hawking again.

I paused as I neared the house. Pre-NORA records said the home was 128 years old. The fact that we had a roof and an actual floor made us richer than most of the Shadows' occupants. I even had a mattress to myself.

But it wasn't the house that made me hesitate. It was its owner. Uncle Dane, leader of the Firebrands, waited at the front door. His shirt hung half buttoned, one pocket slung out of his trousers. He held a packet of alcohol in one hand. I'd planned on quickly changing into my work uniform, but by the self-satisfied expression on his face, there would be no quick retreat today.

"You got an invitation to Neuromen, boy," he said, blocking the doorway as I approached. "Hope you didn't intend to keep that a secret from me."

Anger flared in my chest. Only parents were supposed to receive copies of our official position invitations. That right should have gone to Mom, not him. That meant he'd submitted a request for parental rights while Mom lay in the hospital.

It also meant he knew about the management position.

I schooled my face into innocence like always. "Of course not, Uncle. I meant to tell you today."

"Good. I also hope you intend to accept."

My stomach was boiling now. I briefly considered leaving without my work uniform. My manager already thought the other company foolish for offering me such a high-paying job right out of school. Arriving late would only bring on the taunting. "We'd better discuss this tonight. I'm late for my shift."

My uncle looked nearly identical to my father when he was angry. He'd even shaved his head in Dad's honor, displaying near-constant beads of sweat around what was once his hairline. "We'll discuss it now, *nephew*. A position at Neuromen is a hundred times more important than some lower-management factory job."

Most people would have agreed, but they would be wrong. The factory assembled the circuit boards critical to the nation's neurotechnological communications—an industry that had exploded in recent years. Management positions like mine only opened up every other decade. While Neuromen would have been a huge honor, many of their scientists were permanent assistants with low pay. The factory meant a bigger paycheck from day one. With Mom's hospital bills mounting, that was what mattered.

Except that I couldn't point that out. The less Dane thought about Mom, the better. I was already treading dangerous ground by not immediately obeying his orders. Everything inside me wanted to cower, to lower my head and apologize. Normally I would have done just that.

But not today. Not with my future at stake.

I chose my words carefully. "It was nice of Director Virgil to offer, but I've already committed to the factory. They're expecting me tomorrow night."

"You've committed to nothing until your Declaration, and I say you're taking the lab position."

I pushed past him and stalked down the hallway toward my room. The floorboards creaked underfoot, and I had to squint to find my way in the darkness. Dane rarely paid the electric bill these days. "I'll think about it."

His voice was low and dangerous. "Don't turn your back on me."

With an internal groan, I slowed and turned to face him. "Did you need something else before I leave, Uncle?"

He approached like a panther, slow and deliberate, as if considering how to devour me whole. It was this side of him that ignited the city's discontent with his cause. Anger made my uncle a powerful man. With that power came certain expectations about his family, and unfortunately for me, I was his favorite pawn.

"I'll say it again so you don't misunderstand," he said. "If you care about that sweet, sickly mother of yours, you will accept the lab's offer."

There it was—the weapon I'd dreaded most. He hadn't forgotten about Mom. Her medically induced coma was all that held the brain sickness at bay. All he'd have to do was unplug her, and she'd be gone in a matter of hours.

Dread replaced the heat gathering inside me. "You would threaten a dying woman? Your own sister-in-law?"

"My brother is dead. Now she's nothing to this family. If she's anything to you, you'll stop arguing and listen. That invitation came at the perfect time. I need a man at Neuromen. Unfortunately, you'll have to do."

"You already have a guy working there."

"He defected. I've taken care of it."

Dead, then. "But you have hundreds of followers. Any one of them could spy for you."

"Workers are tracked too closely. Only a neurotech candidate has the right clearance." Alcohol flavored the centimeters between us. "You're the first and only Firebrand graduate with an official invitation."

My teeth were grinding so hard my jaw hurt. After four years on an implant assembly line, I understood neurotech better than any other Firebrand. I was the logical choice.

Swearing under my breath, I realized no argument

would sway Dane now. I agreed with the Firebrand cause. I truly did. But since my father's death last year and Dane's appointment in his place, the cause had degenerated from peaceful protests to violent and dangerous demonstrations, underground work, and bribery. He'd even managed secret infiltrations of Hawking's cabinet. It was only a matter of time before Uncle Dane succeeded in bringing the Rating system back.

If he was right, the change would bring much needed government-paid medical care for Mom, a stable home for all working citizens, and regulated pay for pretty much everyone in the Shadows. Maybe even twenty-four-hour electricity instead of nightly blackouts that only ever seemed to affect those who needed it most. Above all, it meant the nation's ruler was accountable to us and not the other way around. Bloodline ruler mandates and successorships came straight from European histories. They had no place in the New Order Republic of America.

I just wanted to watch it all from a distance. Someone else could be Dane's little pawn.

"Declarations are permanent," I reminded Dane. "To recall it later, I'd have to get a pardon from Hawking himself. We both know that isn't likely to happen." Not when Hawking's own daughter had already figured out I was a Firebrand.

My uncle exhaled, the sour alcohol practically overwhelming my senses. "Boy, I'm saving you from yourself. Decades of barking orders to an assembly line? Even your mama wouldn't want that for you. This lab position will be just the beginning."

I caught the implication. Serve my uncle, rise in the ranks. It was the same offer I'd heard him whisper to other young, ambitious Firebrands. The fact that he would entrust such an important mission to me should have been flattering. Instead, I felt like a bird whose cage had just been opened—only to slam shut a second later. "What intel are you looking for, exactly?"

"There are rumors of an upcoming announcement. Before he . . . left, my man said it's related to the next implant upgrade. I need you to get me details about why this particular update is unique."

It probably patched weaknesses in the system and increased security, like all the others. Dane was crazy. "I believe in the cause, but I can't change the trajectory of my life for a mission someone else could accomplish in a single day. I'm sorry." I turned and headed for my bedroom, determined to grab *all* of my belongings. I wouldn't be returning tonight, or ever.

A hand grabbed me by the collar, tearing my shirt, and yanked me back around. A powerful uppercut took me square in the chin.

I staggered backward against my bedroom door, which gave way, then took a couple of steps before regaining my footing. I knew better than to fall at this man's feet.

Uncle Dane stood in the doorway now, fists still clenched. "Told you never to turn your back on me, fool boy. Thought your dad would've taught you better. I'm not lying. You walk out that door for some stupid factory job and your mama won't survive the night."

There was a lot I hated about my life, but one thing I resented above all—my uncle would win today, and we both knew it. There had been too many dangerous missions under the light of the moon, too many secret conversations overheard. Too many times where he'd demanded and I'd given in. I was my father's son. The blood Dane and I shared put me in a position to be used.

There was just one consolation. Dane wasn't the only one with secrets. If he knew mine, he would have used it today. That, or killed me outright.

I lowered my head like I had a hundred times before and murmured an apology, hating every second of it.

"Good. And you'll declare for Neuromen tomorrow?"

"Yes," I choked out.

He simply swung the packet of alcohol to his mouth and walked away.

I glanced at my black work uniform, pressed and folded neatly on my mattress. It was the only clean thing I owned, a huge contrast to the clutter and disorganization around it. It sat there staring back at me. Mocking my fate.

In one swift movement, I sent it flying across the room. It slid down the wall and landed in a satisfying heap.

THREE
LEGACY

"Legacyyyy," Carmen, Gram's assistant, cried as I walked into Gram's front lobby. The woman crossed her legs and gave a crooked half curtsy that looked more like she had to use the washroom than anything. "What a fun surprise." Translation: *You didn't message me a warning. Again.*

"How is she?" I asked, heading for the stairs, which curved upward in an understated, elegant fashion that reminded me of Gram.

"It's a good day. She may even be awake. Why don't you wait here? I'll go—"

"Don't bother. I'll check in on her." I jogged up the steps and hurried down the hall. I was more familiar with Gram's house than my own—she'd lived here for decades, and our family palace was only a few years old—but I could have found Gram's room by the obnoxious smell of Carmen's perfume alone.

It was better than the antiseptic smell of two years ago, though, when Grandpa Vance had suffered from the brain sickness. Since then it had taken hundreds of lives and earned itself a name as cold as the disease itself—DNR-6.

Like a lightning bolt, his sudden death had shot a crack through our family. He was the one who calmed arguments and soothed hurt feelings. While Gram had shaped a country, Grandpa Vance had shaped our family. His absence made everything feel wrong.

Then Mom died just ten months later. It had widened the crack like a prybar.

Dad had gone into an emotional tailspin, turning his duties over to his cabinet and spending three weeks in his chambers. Gram visited him once, intending to cheer him, but eventually stormed out without explanation. They hadn't spoken since.

Meanwhile, my twin brother, Alex, and I had been left to grieve alone. Alex clung to Dad like never before and refused to talk about Mom. Her belongings and decorations began to disappear.

I finally gathered what remained and hid it in my room.

The hardest part was the conspiracy theories. People claimed horrible things, like Gram murdering her husband and then her daughter-in-law for discovering her guilt. Now, they said, she refused to do the decent thing and follow Grandpa Vance into death. Others accused Dad of killing his own father before staging Mom's "accident." Some even insisted Alex had grown impatient for the successorship and become a murderer.

Then there was the occasional remark about me and my avoidance of the cameras. Surely that meant I was guilty of something.

Gram's door was simple, practical, and to the point. I slid inside and closed it behind me.

My grandmother lay still in her oversized bed, the room dark enough to set me blinking. I felt a stab of guilt. Maybe I should have let her sleep. But tomorrow was Declaration

Day, and Mom wasn't here to talk to. Gram was the next best thing.

She stirred and groaned. "Ugh. That woman's perfume. Open the window, please."

I strode to the window and lifted the shade. Only a sliver of blue sky remained, squeezed out of existence by the usual low-hanging gray clouds. Gram said gray was better than the brown skies and red sun she'd grown up with. I couldn't imagine it.

I took her hand. "How are you feeling today?"

"Cold. I wish they'd give me enough blankets around here. I'm not young anymore." Gram's eyes crinkled, unable to hide the light they always held. She wore her faded brown hair piled atop her head today, held in place with old-fashioned pins and highlighting her slender neck. A threadlike necklace hung crooked down her chest, its stone hidden in her bosom.

I had to agree with Carmen, much as I disliked the woman. It was a good day.

I plucked the top blanket between two fingers in mock disgust. "You're right. Six is woefully inadequate. I mean, don't they know who you are? You deserve at least eight."

"It's true. Now, tell me what's on your mind. You look like you bear the weight of a country on those little shoulders. I know plenty about that. Is your father finally going to announce which of you he's chosen as his successor?"

A tiny smile grew on my lips. She was teasing again. "That happens when we turn eighteen. You're the one who set it up that way, as I recall." Not that there was any question who Dad would choose. Alex had claimed the role of favorite child from the start. "My Declaration, however, is tomorrow."

"I know. Tell me what you're going to say."

I gave her a sideways look. "You're the one who made it illegal to discuss our offers and Declarations. You said it messed up the ratios and made people change their minds when they shouldn't."

She raised a finger and pointed it at my chest. "I said a lot of things. To the fates with all of it. The cursed physician won't let me come tomorrow, so you'd best tell me now."

I swallowed, feeling oddly emotional. My dad, my brother, my aunts and cousins—none of them had ever asked what I intended to Declare. Yet Gram acted like I had a choice. Wrong as it was, it was really, really nice.

"Dad's holding a position for me. Something about research." I hadn't asked for details. All I knew was it involved a desk, a closed door, and the typical long hours that came with a government job. Now my family could avoid each other while getting paid for it.

"That's not what I asked. I want your Declaration. The full version, enthusiasm and all."

The version I was supposed to be practicing with my tutor right now. "It's not ready yet."

"Then you chose wrong, because Declarations aren't written in your mind. They come from the heart."

Not mine. It was more of an "every other door is closed to me" situation. I forced a smile and gave her hand a squeeze. "I'll work on it."

"See that you do. Then come back and give me a proper Declaration. Do me a favor and bring more blankets when you return."

If she wore any more blankets, the poor woman would be folded in half from the weight. I nodded, not quite ready to leave. "Did you want to go into politics?"

She snorted. "Fates, no. It was the last thing I wanted."

"But you didn't have a choice."

A pause. "Well, yes and no. We didn't get to decide our own careers back then, but revolutions have a way of shaking things up. I chose to lay my own plans aside and save people who needed saving."

"Which you did. Got rid of the Rating system, gave power back to the masses." Established the oh-so-critical bloodline of Hawking succession. The Rating system, though, was hard to imagine—people walking around with numbers implanted in their foreheads, judged and paid by what they contributed to society. Or rather, what someone *else* thought they contributed. A twisted system, the thought of which never failed to give me chills.

"My life's work," Gram said. "Not to say I don't have regrets."

She'd never told me this before. "You do?"

"Of course." She squeezed my hand again, her eyes crinkling in amusement. "Governments and laws come and go. They'll absorb every spare second you give them. But you only get one family. When your Grandpa Vance went —" Her voice grew strained, and she cleared her throat. "I don't think Malachite will ever forgive me for the long hours I spent at the office."

Dad hated that name. The only place I'd seen it displayed was on the plaque outside his door and his birth records. He went by Malachi with pretty much everyone who didn't call him "Your Honor."

"I don't see him much more than you do," I grumbled. He'd gone from weeks of isolation to a furious crusade to take down Neuromen Labs.

"Malachite didn't have the best examples of parenting. I let myself become too busy, and Vance tried, but . . . well, our son turned out well regardless. He's doing a lot of good where he is. At the very least, he understands why the Rating system must remain in the ashes of history, which is more than I can say for our vulture neighbors in Malrain and those horrid Fireblood people." She grimaced.

They were *Firebrands*, but I didn't correct her. Nor did I mention that I'd spoken with one of those "horrid people" just this afternoon. All that mattered to my family was the Hawking creed—country over family, country over self. *Hawkings do what is required.* It was a favorite saying of Dad's.

"Is that what you and Dad fought about, then?" I asked, changing the subject. "Dad's upbringing and responsibilities?"

Gram frowned. "Don't you worry about that. Just a little argument that will be resolved in time."

I leaned back in my chair, disappointed. Whatever the cause, neither was willing to budge on their position. Both were equally stubborn in their avoidance of the other.

Gram straightened. "You look so sad. You really don't want to work for your father, do you?"

I pressed my lips together. "I don't know where else I would go."

"You haven't allowed yourself to explore. You have more freedom than you think."

"I wish that were true."

"You're far more than a famous last name. Did you know your mother was an unknown scientist before Malachite ever found her? Yet the people fell instantly in love with her grace, her wit and courage, her intelligence. The accident that took her life devastated the entire country."

I tore my hand from hers and stepped back. "Mom's death was *not* an accident."

Gram sighed and let it go. "You have so much to offer,

Legacy. Don't allow anyone to limit your potential, even yourself."

"I'm not limiting anything. It's like Dad says—I'm a Hawking, and I'll do what's required."

"Tomorrow, you'll do what's *right*," she corrected. "That is, what's right for you. Not what's right for Malachite or Alex or anybody else. Not in this case."

She didn't understand, and I didn't want to argue. "I have to meet the tutor. I hope you feel better soon. Will you be watching on the IM-NET tomorrow, at least?"

Gram made a sour face. "Implants were creepy in Europe when I was young, and they're just as creepy here. I don't care how safe they say it is. No medic is implanting a chip in my mind."

That pulled a grin from me. I'd forgotten how much she hated the things. "I'll see you the day after, then." Working at the Block just a few kilometers from Gram was one benefit of Dad's position. Perhaps the only benefit.

"Day after tomorrow. If the weather improves, there's something I'd like to show you not far from here."

I eyed her blankets. "Will you be feeling up to it?"

"This is worth a little exhaustion. Besides, sea air is more healing than a hundred dark and smelly bedrooms." She pinned me with a flat stare. "Go practice that Declaration of yours. From the heart this time."

FOUR

LEGACY

"What I want to know," Dad said that night at dinner, "is how you arrived an hour late for your tutoring appointment. You could have walked home faster than that." He clutched his fork in one hand and his napkin in the other, his food untouched.

I'd known this was coming the moment I got home and found the tutor gone and Alex wearing a knowing grin. Some twins were best friends. We were anything but. His life's purpose, besides becoming Dad's successor, was to point out every shortcoming I'd ever had.

Well, I sought out opportunities to return the favor often enough, but that was beside the point.

"I have no defense," I said, stabbing my fake pork and shoving it into my mouth.

"You won't even tell me where you went?"

"It's teenage stuff."

"Legacy," Alex said in an exasperated tone that mirrored our father's. "Dad had a tough day at the office. Don't make it worse."

"He always has tough days. I think the term 'tough day'

is in the contract. Strangely, we aren't allowed the same luxury."

Alex pounded his fist on the table, making my silverware jump. "When will you figure out that everything isn't about you? While you're busy failing your classes and avoiding your responsibilities, Dad and I have been dealing with important matters. Like running a country."

"You're right. Those statistics you gathered about the ratio of males versus females in the cattle population of Farming Sector 21 seemed pretty critical."

His face reddened.

Dad cleared his throat. He still hadn't touched his pork. "Don't change the subject, Legacy. You're paying for that lost hour of the tutor's time. He had to reschedule his entire day."

All to practice a one-minute speech I didn't even write. I would read the blasted thing straight from my implant memory files, for fates' sake. I'd been reading since I was four.

"Sorry," I murmured.

Dad set his fork down and massaged his temple. "The tabloids ran my segment for weeks after my Declaration. They scrutinized every word. Every *inflection* of every word. They'll do the same to you two simply because you're a Hawking. If anything, it'll be worse. It's been a slow news week."

"I don't know why they care," I said. "It's not like it's any surprise what we're going to announce."

"We serve the public. Just like your grandmother, just like your grandfather. I accepted my responsibility, and your—" Dad choked and cleared his throat again. He was about to mention Mom. He hadn't made that mistake in months. "It's what you'll both do as well, particularly the one who becomes my successor. Those we serve respect that sacrifice and honor it every way they can. The least you can do is acknowledge the privilege you've been given and do as required."

Alex nodded vigorously, as if Dad had said something profound. I barely contained an eye roll. Gram's edict about the Honorship following the Hawking bloodline may have answered the long-term successorship question, but she obviously hadn't considered the possibility of twins. Alex grew more unbearable by the hour.

Dad finally pushed his plate away. "Let's discuss tomorrow's Declaration. Your drivers will bring you to the park fifteen minutes early. I'll meet you there later. The public tour of your new offices is scheduled for an hour after the ceremony ends. I expect you both to be there, smiling and presentable."

"Can't wait." Alex shoved another bite into his mouth.

From one prison to another, indeed. "Yes, Dad."

He slumped against his chair and began rubbing at his temple again. "I'm going to bed early. Practice your speeches until you're hoarse. It's hard to keep your wits when you have fifteen cameras aimed at your face."

I almost blurted out how eager I was to investigate cow-gender ratios and make a difference in the world, but the words died on my lips. Dad always looked tired, but today he looked truly exhausted. "What happened at the office today?"

Alex snorted. "Oh, now you're interested."

"Nothing too drastic," Dad began. "Just more drama with Neuromen. The committee clings so tightly to Virgil's promises they can't see how dangerous that place is." He sighed. "I just want to be done with all of this."

I stabbed a piece of pork and dragged it around my

plate, any appetite gone. Dad should have received a copy of my official Neuromen invitation today, but he hadn't raised the subject at all. He was probably too distracted to notice. Fates knew he had enough messages to deal with these days, and the Neuromen invitation was only one of fifty I'd received.

I hesitated, then plunged in. "Dad, I've been wondering something. Do you want Neuromen shut down because it's dangerous for everyone or just because of Mom?"

Dad flinched. To my surprise, Alex withheld the lecture this time. He watched Dad as closely as I did.

"That's a fair question," Dad finally said. "I've asked myself that many times, and I think it's a combination of both. I never liked Director Virgil's secrecy, particularly since he receives government research funds. I always had a weird feeling about the man. Paranoid one second, oblivious the next. When he appointed your mom as head of his research department, I decided not to voice my concerns to her. She was so happy." He paused. "I should have said something."

He fell silent. Alex and I exchanged a long look. We were accustomed to silence these days, and he rarely opened up like this. Dad hadn't allowed us to discuss anything meaningful in almost a year.

I decided to push one last time. "Mom's death wasn't an accident, was it?"

"*Legacy*," Alex snapped. "What's the matter with you?"

"I'm about to commit my entire life and future to family politics. I'm right, and I think Dad knows it."

Dad's set down his fork, looking haunted. It was as if I'd lifted my steak knife and stabbed him in the heart. But there was something else in his eyes that made me swallow hard.

"I'll see you both tomorrow," he said. Then he practically launched himself out the door.

I stared at his empty chair. I'd expected sorrow, perhaps, or even anger at the question. But his eyes held something chilling, an emotion I couldn't have predicted in a decade.

Guilt.

"Now look what you did," Alex snapped.

I whirled on him. "Leave. Me. Alone."

My brother sat back in his chair, a barely contained anger in his eyes. "You have no idea what real life is like, do you? Just your own selfish little world."

"Politics hardly qualify as the real world."

He shoved another bite into his mouth, half chewed it, and swallowed. "It doesn't matter how she died. It won't bring her back."

"I'm not stupid. I know that. But knowing will help us all move on. Don't you ever wonder what really happened to her?"

"No, and you shouldn't either. She made a dumb mistake and blew herself up. Dad and I have already moved on. I don't see why you can't."

The anger grew inside me. It had made an appearance that terrible day over a year ago, and it wasn't any smaller after a year of crippling grief. If anything, it had flared into a raging volcanic inferno. Something told me it would simmer the rest of my life if I didn't get the answers I needed. "You two pretend Mom never existed, but that's not moving on. That's betrayal."

"People die all the time, Legacy. It's a part of life." Another massive bite.

I gaped at my brother. *A part of life?* The twin I'd grown up with felt like a stranger these days. We'd spent our early years following each other around in search of mischief.

Some of my favorite memories were of us making mud together and painting the kitchen—and each other—in nut paste. As we grew older, we'd raced around the trees surrounding our estate. Alex usually won, but my occasional victory fueled me enough to keep trying. It had been years since our last race.

The change in Alex had been the most glaring at Mom's memorial session. Alex wore white like Dad and me, but that was where the resemblance ended. He'd spent every minute making jokes, interviewing for the cameras, and posing for captures with the guests. No wonder people thought we were a family of heartless murderers.

That was the heritage I belonged to now. Expectations, avoidance, and downright silence. I felt no pride in any of it. Just a strangling sensation.

I shoved my still-full plate toward him, nearly launching it off the table. He caught it at the last second. Then I stomped out.

When I reached my room, full of furniture I never used and colors I'd never actually liked, I stalked to the window and opened it. Cold night air entered immediately, cooling my flushed skin. Through the branches of my favorite bigleaf maple glowed the nearly full moon—a bright yet gentle constant in a life that felt increasingly turbulent. Gram loved the warm days of summer, but it was the night that drew me toward its welcoming embrace. Light meant people and judgment and pointing fingers. Darkness meant solitude. The fates knew how little I got of that these days.

Unfortunately, the moon also reminded me of Mom.

I plopped onto my bed, pointedly avoiding the spot where Mom always sat during our late-night talks, and pulled up Virgil's message again.

Mom had received one of these at my age. Unlike me,

she actually worked hard for it. She'd approached life like a scientist, in a logical and mathematical way. She was relentless at her job, focused in a way I'd never been at anything. Except, perhaps, avoiding my family.

I blinked a few times, pulling up our last family capture. On our seventeenth birthday, Mom had arranged for a day away from the city. She'd even convinced Dad to come. We'd gone hiking in the hills and eaten lunch at an old wooden table. It wasn't until we'd returned to the oversized family transport that the driver forever captured the moment.

Mom walked between Alex and me, her arm around each of our shoulders and laughing. Flushed from the exercise, pink from the sun, she looked radiant. Utterly, unquestioningly happy. Dad walked behind us, watching her with a tiny smile. I returned Mom's gaze with an amused expression, my hand steadying her arm as if unwilling to let it go. Alex, not surprisingly, scowled at the ground.

That chunk of heat inside me began to glow brighter.

There was a huge difference between accident and murder. Alex was wrong. It absolutely mattered.

It was the thing that mattered most.

I locked the door, deleted my tutor's scripted speech, and began one of my own.

FIVE

LEGACY

Fifty years ago, things had been very different. Graduates gathered at assemblies to be given a Rating for implantation, the numbers they wore their entire lives thereafter changing at the government's whim. Those who were deemed obedient lived rich and easy lives. The disobedient suffered. All these historical tidbits I'd memorized along with my statistics and literature facts.

Today's version was far less intense on the slap-a-number-on-you front. Companies were required to take on a certain number of new graduates and fought over the most promising and hardworking candidates. Those who received no invitations filled openings in the less desirable fields. No number surgery required.

Now we had to actually get to know people—a blessing and a curse.

Another difference was the venue. Rather than being told in a cold auditorium where we'd spend our lives, graduates Declared their choices on platforms erected in public parks all over the country. Camera crews arrived hours early, while broadcasting stations gossiped about our potential. For a single day, seventeen-year-old graduates held the attention of a nation.

I watched fifteen minutes' worth of IM-NET newscast gossip as we lined up on the platform. Alex's face appeared dozens of times, inevitably followed by mine. I changed the station every time. I knew about the Firebrands' petition to deny me Dad's position based on my disappointing performance in school, but they hadn't won. I almost wished they had. It would make my day a whole lot easier.

A capture of Kole the Firebrand's face appeared on a lesser-known station. I turned up my internal volume. The female commentator speculated about his experience in some tech factory, calling him "one of the more promising candidates despite his upbringing." I laughed aloud at that. They didn't realize how dangerous his upbringing truly was.

The commentator's partner, a woman with poufy, too-bright-red hair simply laughed and dismissed the opinion with a wave. "Kole Mason hails from the Shadows. He'll be a disappointment like all the others."

Ouch.

I looked past the screen overlay and scanned the platform, looking for Kole's head of nearly black hair and wondering if he was even watching. I found him near the back, scowling at the ground. At least he wasn't breaking character for the event.

A stir of anticipation went through the crowd. 09:00. Time to begin.

The school director motioned Alex and me forward, her pleasant demeanor betraying no hint of the irritation I'd caused her over the past three years. Alex would go first, of course. I situated myself next to my brother and pasted on my public smile for the cameras while resenting every single one. If only our Declarations could happen off-screen. My hand accidentally brushed his arm.

Alex went rigid and stepped to the side, placing distance between us. He hadn't forgiven me for last night. Fine. I hadn't forgiven him either.

The director gave a short speech about our Declarations, what they meant, and our potential to change the world or some such nonsense. Then she addressed the graduates, advising us to choose carefully. If we later regretted our choice of career, it would take an order from my father himself to reverse it—and he didn't often grant those. It was a policy I happened to agree with. It would ruin the system to make exceptions all the time.

Finally, it was Alex's turn. The park went quiet as he stepped forward.

"I'm Alexandrite Hawking, firstborn of His Honorable Malachite Hawking. I'm pleased to accept his invitation of an Honor Fellowship. I thank you again for your undying support."

I managed not to gag while the audience applauded. *Firstborn. Honor Fellowship.* It was like he wanted to beat me over the head with the words. Throwing Dad's name where it didn't belong would only irritate people. Besides, only Hawking supporters gave us "undying support." Over a third of the country disapproved of Dad's policies. If Alex didn't realize that, he truly was delusional about *real life*.

He stepped back, and I took his place, pulling up the mental file I'd created last night. The words floated in my vision in dark letters. Every set of eyes was on me now. Dad stood near the back of the crowd before us, surrounded by his bodyguards and probably being orbited by several more in civilian attire. His expression took a chunk out of my resolve. He looked happy for the first time in months.

I tugged at my deep-silver dress, chosen from Mom's closet. She'd let me borrow it last year. "It complements your green eyes and dark hair," she'd said.

She should be here.

My eyes suddenly went raw. I blinked the pain away as the applause died out.

"I'm Legacy Hawking," I began, trying desperately not to let my voice wobble. "Daughter of Malachite *and* Andreah Hawking. I'm afraid I won't be taking the second Honor Fellowship position with Alex as originally planned. I've decided to accept the invitation of Director Virgil at Neuromen Labs instead."

I'd expected dramatic gasps, but the entire crowd just went rigid and still. Dad's face drained of color. His eyes were two round, dark spots against a startlingly white canvas.

"I'm eager to continue the work my mother died to bring into the world," I continued, my voice pleading now as if addressing Dad. "I realize that there's tension between the program and the government, but until that's resolved, I'd like to contribute what I can." A pause. That last part hadn't been planned, but it felt right. "Thank you."

I stepped back, allowing the next graduate to take my place. It was over. I felt limp. My family wouldn't understand, but I would find the answers Dad refused to give. I would discover the truth if it took a lifetime.

I barely heard the next graduate's Declaration. "I, Aada Clarinn, declare my intention to enter the civil engineering field. I'd like to thank my family . . ."

Dad was already gone. He'd slipped into the crowd. Gone back to the office? Recovering from his shock in a transport? It was impossible to know.

Slowly, cautiously, I pulled up a few broadcasting

stations. One displayed an unflattering capture of myself just seconds earlier, my mouth gaped in speech. I decided not to turn up the volume.

Several more graduates Declared, followed by a girl with extremely short black hair that emphasized her slender neck and smoky-quartz-brown skin. I knew her vaguely from my science classes.

"Amelia 'Millian' Comondor, at your service," she said with a tilted curtsy to the crowd.

I hid a grin. *At your service?* Now I remembered why most of our graduating class laughed behind her back. *Millian*, like the number, only spelled wrong. She posed like a queen for the cameras despite her mismatched outfit. It almost made me like her.

"I'm pleased to announce that I, too, am joining Neuromen Labs."

My breath caught. It hadn't occurred to me that others might choose the same path. I did a quick search for graduates who'd declared for Neuromen and found only a half dozen across the country so far, all top students with a science emphasis. I shifted my weight. Most of the public knew how terrible my science grades had been. Were they laughing at me as much as at Millian?

I dismissed the IM-NET, letting the overlay screen disappear. Let them think what they wanted. Virgil had invited me, and I'd made my choice.

The Firebrand went several minutes later. "Kole Mason, declaring for Neuromen as well." He stepped back and buried himself in line, his scowl deeper than before.

I blinked. How had a boy from the Shadows received an official invitation? Why would he even accept? Surely he was too busy dreaming of massive government overhauls to care about his future.

I thought back to the earlier broadcast and their musing about his lack of potential. Something to prove? An attempt to climb out of poverty? The timing of all this certainly was suspect. Our argument yesterday, and now he was following me to Neuromen. The two couldn't be related, could they? I ground my teeth in frustration. Obviously I'd missed something.

Kole must have felt my eyes on him because he met my gaze with a hard stare of his own.

I tore my eyes away and focused on the next graduate, hoping my heated cheeks weren't noticeable. I was Legacy Hawking, granddaughter of Her Honorable Treena Hawking. I didn't much care what a random Firebrand did or why.

Meanwhile, I allowed myself the tiniest swell of victory. I'd done it. My family's expectations no longer had a hold on my life. I felt Alex's eyes boring into me, but it didn't matter now. For the first time in my life, I was completely and utterly free.

"CAN you tell us why you changed your mind?" the reporter asked.

I fought to remain focused on the man's face, a hard feat considering Kole was being interviewed just three meters away. He spoke quietly, thoughtfully. If I hadn't argued with him just yesterday, I'd believe he was a gentle and intelligent graduate headed off to a bright future.

Good thing I knew better.

"Miss Hawking? Are you okay?"

I blinked and glanced at the camera. Oh, there were three on me now. "Yeah. My mom believed in her research, and I do too. I'm pleased to be offered an opportunity to continue the work she started."

"Have you always had your eye on the science field?"

"Not at all. But sometimes you just have to go your own way."

"An admirable view, Miss Hawking, especially considering your test results don't show an aptitude for science. Do you hope to overcome that stigma during Training Week?"

My eyes narrowed as the reporter waited expectantly. I was a fool for hoping the subject wouldn't come up. Of course the press had my aptitude-test results. "I'm honored that Director Virgil saw my potential. I intend to overcome anything that stands in my way."

Kole's interview ended. He strode away without thanking the reporters. Then the crowd parted, and my dad was there.

"Thank you," the reporter said quickly, drawing back to give us a little privacy. The cameras, however, continued to roll.

I'd expected Dad to grab my arm and yank me through the audience like a child, lecturing me all the while about telling them I'd made a mistake. One word, and he could order my choice revoked. But he just stood there in his best suit, his collar uncharacteristically askew and his chest moving up and down like it took a monumental effort to breathe.

Then he wrapped me in his arms.

I felt my eyes go wide as my body stiffened. Dad hadn't hugged me since . . . I couldn't even remember. Long before Mom's funeral, where he'd stood rooted like his feet were part of the earth. His arms trembled. Slowly, mechanically, I lifted my arms to pat his back.

"You don't know what you've done," he whispered into my hair, his voice muffled. "This can't be taken back. It can't . . . you can't . . ." With a cry, he tore away and walked off.

The cameras followed him, leaving me alone.

Alex approached from somewhere and applauded. "It's official. You're an idiot."

I kept my eyes on Dad. The reporter was one step behind him, shouting questions at his back. "Is he okay?"

"He lost Mom to a huge explosion. Now you're headed to the same lab without the scientific expertise Mom had. You'll be completely reliant on the one man Dad hates with all his being. So no, he's not okay."

"I didn't want to hurt him."

"Yeah? Well, you did."

I stepped back, putting space between us. "The transport will be here soon. Will you tell him I'll miss him? And that I won't let anything happen to me. And tell him . . . tell him I'm going to discover the truth."

Alex groaned. "You've got to be kidding."

I flinched. "I understand what Dad thinks of Virgil, but—"

"What Dad *knows* of him. He's going to use you, Legacy. Just like he used Mom."

"Let him try."

He sighed and held out a hand. "Seems like you've made up your mind, then. Good luck."

Feeling a distant camera on us, I gripped his hand and gave it a hard shake. Inside, I was puzzled. A handshake? What were we, work partners?

My twin shrugged and strode off, his attention already captured by something—or someone—at the edge of the crowd.

Something was off. He'd given up too easily. No

farewell, no offers to keep in touch. It was almost as if he were relieved.

Of course he was glad. If there was ever a question of who Dad would announce as his successor on our next birthday, there wasn't now. Good. Let him follow Dad around like a good little lapdog. I had other plans.

A message scrolled across my vision.

ALL NEUROMEN RECRUITS: HEAD TO THE SOUTHEAST TRANSPORT LOT FOR YOUR ASSIGNED PICKUP.

The other graduates must have also received pickup instructions from their respective companies because an excited cry rose from the crowd. Families hugged each other through smiles and tears. Friends offered promise-filled goodbyes. I'd hoped to say goodbye to Travers, but he was nowhere to be seen.

I folded my arms, suddenly feeling very much alone. Mom would have hugged me to the very last second and escorted me to the transport, discussing how exciting it would be to work together.

At least Gram would approve. Carmen was likely telling her right now, raging about my choice while Gram looked on with a knowing smile.

Across the crowd, Kole shuffled his feet, looking every bit as alone as I felt. No family members or friends had shown up to see him off. At least he hadn't gotten lectures and guilt trips about *his* choice.

Straightening, I turned my back on the platform and the reporters and all that remained of my former life. Then I marched toward destiny.

SIX

KOLE

I WAITED until the last second to join the others on the transport, half hoping Dane would come running onto the trampled grass and say he didn't need me after all. Not that it would have mattered. My management position at the factory would be filled by someone else before I even reached the lab.

The transport was simple and unmarked—four-seater, plain gray interior, huge tinted windows. I appreciated the discretion. Riding to my new job in some flamboyant, Neuromen-logo-riddled vehicle would have been too much. A pretty blonde escort with tightly bound hair sat impatiently at the front.

I plopped into the only seat available, the one across from a moody Legacy Hawking, and flung my night bag between us. She glared out the window while braiding her dark hair over one shoulder, eyes glazed over. Probably watching herself being discussed on the IM-NET. I didn't get her at all. Was this a cry for attention or simply a way to piss her dad off? I was willing to bet it had nothing to do with "continuing where Mom left off" or whatever.

I didn't check the IM-NET myself. Any theories people had about me were wrong and irrelevant.

Legacy's presence would complicate things. Any minute, my uncle would discover the heiress's Declaration and devise a new slew of plans to use her. This time, I couldn't just tell him no. His house was only twenty minutes from Mom's hospital room, and Neuromen was an hour's transport ride. Until I earned enough to move Mom to a closer hospital, I was pure Firebrand puppet material.

Next to the blonde woman sat a black-haired girl I recognized from school. She had a strange name. Thousand or something. She knelt to peer over the seat at us.

"Hate to interrupt the brooding and all," she said, "but I'm Millian, top scorer in the district in neurotechnology and a huge Virgil fan. I'm taking his job someday. How about you guys?"

I grunted. Legacy kept scowling out the window, though by the clearness of her eyes, she'd at least turned her broadcast off.

Millian rolled her dark-brown eyes. "Fine. Let's do awkward, then. It's not like we'll be living and working together for the rest of our lives or anything." She slid down to face the front again.

Legacy folded her arms to match her slender legs, one crossed over the other. She may as well have a laser sign over her head reading, "Leave me alone or else."

The escort must have received a message of some kind because she turned in her seat with a suddenly bright smile, then said, "Thank you for arriving so promptly. We're pleased to have you. We'll be arriving at Neuromen and your new home in sixty-seven minutes. Enjoy the trip."

New home. I didn't know Legacy's reason for being

here, but it was clear Millian was the only new recruit from our city who was happy with the whole Neuromen thing.

I adjusted my shirt. I'd buttoned it nearly to my neck today to cover the raw patch of skin boasting my new hidden Firebrand tattoo. It burned against the rough cloth. The only consolation was that Mom wouldn't know I'd taken the oath for several more months when she awoke from her coma. Most of our recruits had to wait until their eighteenth birthday. Lucky me.

Traffic from other company transports slowed us getting out of the parking lot, which suited me just fine. I ran through my uncle's orders once again as the park grew smaller in the distance.

Keep an eye on Virgil. The man directed a huge company, so I wasn't sure how easy this would be.

Discover what the new implant update does. I'd start by asking around for information, determining who could be trusted and who couldn't. That was always the most dangerous part.

Don't blow your cover. Legacy Hawking obviously knew what I was, but there was no indication that anyone else did. The longer things stayed that way, the less suspicious I would appear to Director Virgil. Keeping a low profile, giving everyone the illusion of a quiet, obedient teenager, would be essential.

I wasn't a fool. I knew what failure in any of these areas would mean. Not only would I never see my mother alive again, but my standing with the party would be jeopardized. Bad things happened to the Branded when they strayed from the cause.

"You look awfully somber," Legacy muttered, and I wondered how long she'd been watching. "No better options, then?"

"Not exactly."

"They say you turned down a management position with better pay. I'm curious to know why."

I stifled a groan. "While you're throwing judgments around, ask yourself the same question."

"I have my reasons."

"So do I."

"It's a harmless question—"

"Look. I know this is the first time you've been away from Daddy, but just because we'll be working together doesn't mean we're friends. You're still a Hawking, and I'm still . . . who I am. That isn't going to change." Last night's hurried branding ceremony had clinched it forever.

I turned toward the window and away from her. Her gaze burned into my back for a long moment. I pushed away the guilt. Surely an heiress was used to bluntness on occasion. The more distance between me and the Hawkings, the better.

My uncle's web was the last place Legacy wanted to end up.

She chuckled. "Right. Forgive me. I forgot that Firebrands don't believe in common decency." The seat squeaked as she turned away, probably to glare out the window once more.

Right. Common decency like you just gave Millian. The thought gave me little pleasure.

The rest of the ride passed in silence.

SEVEN
LEGACY

I PUSHED Kole's rude response to the back of my mind as the city I'd grown up in shrank in the distance. The drive to the lab was a familiar one—a winding road through forest-land that suddenly opened up into a wide expanse of ocean. A narrow white bridge, wide at the entrance and tapering into a graceful arc, took us over the coastline and onto the island where Neuromen stood. The bay was a brilliant blue below us as the trees disappeared behind.

The inside would have been disappointing if I hadn't seen it before. The lab's stark-white theme was everywhere —on the high ceilings, glossy walls, and even shinier floors. It was like room after room of hardened milk. As always, my stomach flip-flopped for a second as I struggled to get my bearings.

Two things, however, were new. The dizzying ceiling was now broken up by a series of tiny sprinkler heads. If those filled every room in the building, Virgil was deter-mined to halt any new fires before they truly began. The second addition was the neat line of employees with tidy gray uniforms. They greeted the newly arrived graduates, who increased by the minute as transports arrived from various cities. None of the workers wore the white coat of a scientist. We weren't important enough to tear *them* away from their work.

I nodded to the employees as we passed. Some returned the gesture, while others simply examined me curiously. I felt as comfortable as an earthworm in a gull's mouth until one, a woman with graying hair as short as Millian's, gave me a smile and a wink. At least someone here was friendly.

Our escort tapped her way to the front of the group and placed herself next to a darkened window. Sometime between leaving the ceremony and our arrival, she'd pulled her blonde hair into a bun so tight it pinched her eyes. I blinked as a few paragraphs of small white text appeared on the dark glass. A techboard. CONTRACT was visible at the top in bold letters.

"Welcome, our fourteen newest additions to the program," she said cheerfully. "I'm Soren, your escort and friend. Forgive the red tape. Even visitors sign the board, and our recruits—or candidates, as we call them—are far more important than visitors." A strained smile. "Legacy Hawking, our most recognizable candidate. Would you lead us off?"

I swept up to the board, pretended to skim through it, and used my finger to create my signature icon at the bottom—a circle with five connecting lines in the center for my family's crest, then a swiggle to the right ending in a circle. I'd designed the icon at age four, thinking it looked like a magic wand. Now I preferred to think of it as a rising full moon.

Millian, who'd waited impatiently for me to finish, was the next to step up. She signed a series of circles with a flourish, then turned and flashed the crowd a triumphant smile.

Kole avoided my gaze as he stepped up to the board next. After his wretched behavior on the transport, I tried not to act too interested in his icon as he lifted his finger to sign. A boxed-in letter *K* with a spiky design in the bottom right corner. A plant? Not at all what I'd expected from a Firebrand. Surely there should have been a flame full of swords or something equally dramatic.

I recognized the others from the broadcast I'd watched on the way here, all students with a strong science or technology background. Graduates Virgil actually *wanted* here. A worm in a gull's mouth described this moment perfectly.

When all the graduates had signed, Soren unlocked the door. A simple implant-sensitive lock, though from the electric sound inside the door, its mechanism was anything but simple. I stepped through, eager to see a part of the lab I'd never accessed before.

The door led to a long, bright hallway. Sunlight filtered by small, square windows gave the white walls an odd, almost pink hue despite the glass's greenish tint—neoglass, a modern alternative to the breakable kind. Soren set a quick pace for the opposite end, an admirable feat considering the speech she was launching into. Something about the history of the lab and Director Virgil's impressive accomplishments.

I glanced outside as I passed the third window and drew to a stop. A beautiful garden lay outside, though that wasn't what caught my eye. I'd seen plenty of gardens. Behind a tree, partially hidden by branches, stood a wide wall with angry black writing. Workers were scrubbing it off. Graffiti at a science lab?

I squinted, trying to make out the words. Only portions were visible.

Your lies

Will see that

Revenge

Excitement sent my heart racing. This was exactly the kind of thing I'd expected to find here, and we hadn't even reached our quarters yet. I needed a closer look. Given Soren's pace, she knew about it and didn't want us lingering. That meant I had to be very careful not to get caught.

The others were two-thirds of the way down the hallway now, all riveted on the back of Soren's head. She gestured grandly with one hand. Whatever story she was currently telling, she was completely absorbed in it.

There. A door leading outside stood partially ajar, propped open with a bucket of cleaning supplies.

I slid through the opening, blinking in the afternoon sunlight. Two workers dressed in gray janitorial uniforms scrubbed at the wall, chatting in low tones.

I slipped into the shadow of a tree. The workers would see me if they turned around, but at least I was out of sight of that hallway full of fake glass windows.

Pulse hammering, I scurried behind a second tree and then a third, getting closer with each. The first worker had begun to scrub away the word "revenge." My eyes slid to their boots. A blackened can of spray paint lay on the ground. Next to it was a dark smear of red paint.

I squinted. No, that wasn't paint. It had to be—

"Miss Hawking?"

I jumped and turned to see Soren standing in the middle of the garden, one eyebrow raised.

"Yes?" I croaked.

Her eyes swept the wall but kept going, as if she wanted

to pretend nothing was amiss. "There will be time to tour this section later. We haven't programmed any locks with your implant signature yet. You'd best remain with the group to avoid getting yourself locked out."

"Of course." I threw one last glance at the wall to take a quick capture, then hurried past her, feeling my cheeks redden. Did Director Virgil know about the graffiti? Surely such a self-important man made it his business to know. Then again, he'd been oblivious to Mom's experiment before she died. Or at least that's what he'd insisted that night.

Mom was not only dead, he'd told us, but her body had been obliterated in the explosion, nothing left to cremate.

The rest of the group whispered at the end of the hallway as they watched me approach. Kole's eyes lingered the longest as Soren resumed her place at the head of the group and continued her story.

I barely heard it. I wasn't supposed to see that graffiti, and that made it absolutely my business. But it wasn't the message that made my blood race.

That red smear on the floor hadn't been paint. I was certain of it.

————

AN HOUR LATER, after a lecture about the company's rules and expectations, we were sized for new uniforms— not the gray of the workers' clothing, but a deep blue and sporting a gold band across the chest and back—and separated into bunk rooms. I chose the farthest one down the ladies' hall. It stood empty except for two narrow metal beds and a dresser. No sofa. They didn't expect us to do any lounging, it seemed. On the far end of the room was a wash-room barely the size of a small closet.

"Welcome to your new life," I muttered, for once missing my designer bedroom and its hideous furniture.

A new icon appeared in my vision. It outlined the rules again and included a new section on the hierarchy of Neuromen. It was as I'd suspected—there weren't enough scientist positions for all of us. Over half would be assigned assistant positions while only the top five moved on to official neurotech training. Our test results during the next week would determine who went where.

Feeling uneasy, I pulled up today's schedule in a separate icon. Dinner in fifteen minutes, then leisure time in the New Recruit lounge. Testing began tomorrow. I squirmed at that. Even if I knew what to study, it wouldn't do me much good now. I hadn't really expected to climb ranks in the company, but I didn't want to sink to the bottom, either.

I changed into my stiff new uniform, put my clothes away as neatly as they would fit, then plopped onto the hard bed with a grimace.

I pulled up the graffiti capture and grimaced at its poor quality. Regardless, the hurried black words and that red bloodstain screamed against the whiteness surrounding them. The real question was, who was behind the message and what had happened to them? Stunners didn't make a person bleed. New NORA hadn't allowed a weapon that fired bullets in decades. That meant someone could have been stabbed or beaten here. Maybe killed.

I scanned the news reports again without success. No mention of an incident at Neuromen at all. Just the gradu-ates' Declarations today. It was certain, then. Whatever had happened, Virgil wasn't talking.

The bedroom door opened to reveal Millian, an

overnight bag slung over her shoulder. Her smile froze at the sight of me. "Right. Not happening." She stepped back into the hall and slammed the door.

I stared at the door in irritation. Part of me wanted to fling it open and demand she come back and apologize. But that would defeat the whole not-wanting-a-roommate thing.

A few minutes later, the door opened again, a frustrated Millian shoving through it and tossing her bag onto the other bed. Then she stalked into the washroom and closed the door behind her, more gently this time.

"Um," I said. Her bag taunted me from the other bed. "I don't think so."

"That's what I said," she called from the washroom. "Except there are no more open beds. I'd rather sleep in the hall."

"Sounds good. I'll toss a blanket out there for you."

"Nope," she said through the door. "I'm good here. I think the washroom is cleaner than the bedroom anyway."

"You intruded first."

"And you'll eventually need to intrude on my washroom, so we'd better work out some kind of arrangement."

A voice came over the speaker. "All new volunteers, report to the cafeteria in five minutes."

I folded my arms. "They're calling you, nerd."

She emerged from the washroom. "Nope. The moment I leave, you'll throw my stuff out. We're leaving together, oh, buddy of mine." Her medium brown face looked flushed, but by the determined set of her mouth, it wasn't embarrassment. She didn't like this arrangement any better than I did.

"We aren't done discussing this," I told her.

She just rolled her eyes.

Millian did end up leaving first, but only barely. She kept a close eye on me, as if she really did believe I'd run back to the room and toss her junk out. I had to admit it was tempting. But her implant would be registered to the lock too. She was just as likely to throw *my* stuff out.

I looped around to the garden to search for more clues on my way to the cafeteria, but Soren stood at the entrance to the long hallway. She smirked at my attempt to look casual as I circled back to the cafeteria. Everything was likely to be cleaned up by now anyway. I'd have to find another lead.

Dinner was—no surprise—fake meat and vegetables that tasted like they'd taken a chemical bath. I sat at the farthest table from the others and concentrated on not vomiting and, most definitely, *not* looking at Kole. A few sets of eyes glanced curiously at me, but nobody crossed the room. Millian sat as far from my table as possible. Fine by me.

I swallowed, scooped another bite of whatever this was into my mouth, and pulled up the news feeds. An offshoot Firebrands group in West Salem, a city near the border of New NORA and Malrain, had staged a protest outside their city offices today. They complained about having more than their fair share of uninvited graduates. Dad ensured there were always positions in the farming industry and the military, but most weren't thrilled about either. Many of the protestors carried signs about wanting the Rating system back.

I wanted to understand their reasoning, but their solution was one I strongly disagreed with. In too many ways, the old NORA Rating system was still hard-wired into people's brains. Many complained that their children were hungrier than ever, that they struggled to find jobs and housing that fit their fixed incomes. The protests had gotten bigger and more violent in recent months. All the while,

Dad released statements about appreciating our freedom and filed their complaints away for later.

Mom would have listened to them. Of that I was sure. She wouldn't have reinstated the controlling regime they wanted, but she would have listened and sympathized. Yet it was Dad, not Mom, in the Copper Office.

I felt guilty at the thought. I didn't resent Dad for being the parent who remained, but I did resent how distant we'd grown. When we did speak, he felt like a stranger who buried himself in work to avoid feeling anything at all. Better to avoid what remained of his family than recognize that it was now incomplete.

But here, I felt closer to Mom than ever. I looked around the cafeteria and tried to imagine her sitting here on her first day. Had she come determined to make a difference in the world? To invent something that would solve society's problems? To leave a legacy everyone would remember?

If she'd known how it all would turn out, would she still have chosen this?

I tossed what remained of my food and headed back to the room, my determination set. Soren couldn't block that hallway forever. When night fell, I would try again. Then I would explore this place until I knew every centimeter of it.

My official investigation had begun.

EIGHT

KOLE

Nothing about the lab's layout was a surprise, except maybe the center garden. The greenery, combined with its wet-dirt smell and misted air, clashed with the sterile whiteness of Neuromen's little utopia.

Four evenly spaced wings extended from the halls leading to the garden—the candidate dorm and cafeteria wing, a second wing for the scientists, the lab wing, and a fourth with an unmarked door. I imagined the building looked like a giant snowflake from the air. Only the unmarked wing remained locked when I approached, refusing to reveal its secrets.

A tiny red light blinked overhead. Another camera. They hung in every hallway, but this particular corridor held two. It wouldn't surprise me if there were hidden ones too.

Virgil's wing, then. His secret project lay somewhere behind this door.

I gave the entry a sweeping glance, trying not to look too interested for the camera's sake. *Just a simple candidate exploring his new home. Nothing to worry about.*

The door had been painted to resemble the rest, but its too-even surface revealed this one was reinforced. There would be no busting through with sheer force. No visible mechanism or mechanical lock at all, which was consistent with everything else here. It made sense that Virgil would rely on the technology he'd invented. Nobody got through without implant access.

I turned and headed back to the candidate wing, my mind already picking the problem apart. Virgil kept us newbies separate from the rest, which meant it would be difficult to find someone with the authorization to get past this door—let alone convince them to bring me along.

An outdoor entrance, then. There were emergency exits all over this place. Virgil would never leave himself without a means of escape should fire break out, particularly after what had happened with Legacy's mom. They said that half a wing had burned before officials got it under control. Frankly, Virgil was lucky that the other scientists had escaped at all.

I'd just passed the cafeteria to my left when the lights went out. Nightly electricity mandate—a way of life for those from the Shadows. Apparently Hawking had inflicted his stupid energy rules upon the lab, too. Better to remove power from the poor and businesses than use it wisely during the day. Getting rid of all those stupid ad boards would have been a great place to start.

A groan sounded from inside the cafeteria doors.

I froze, then plastered myself against the wall. Stupid. I hadn't considered the possibility that Virgil might send someone to follow me.

A feminine voice muttered some not-so-feminine words, and I felt a grin cross my face. Legacy Hawking. She probably hadn't experienced a blackout mandate in her entire life.

"Midnight snack?" I asked.

I heard her emerge from the doors, following my voice. "Something like that."

"I doubt anyone is in the kitchens this time of night."

She muttered another curse and began walking away, probably feeling her way along the wall. "I suppose you were just getting exercise."

"Something like that."

She hit a wall and grunted.

"You know," I began, determined to enjoy this, "you could wait until the backup lights come on. It should happen any second."

"Stand here in the dark with you? My dream come true."

"You didn't really assume Neuromen's lights would stay on for you all night." I paused. "I take that back. It sounds exactly like something a rich heiress would expect."

"And following a rich heiress around a dark lab at night, spewing taunts at her, is exactly what I'd expect from a Firebrand. You really have nothing better to do?"

"I did, but watching you run into walls is much more fun."

Tiny green lights appeared along the floor, illuminating the edges of the hallway like a long carpet. Legacy's slender legs were visible now, as was her startled stance. She'd assumed I was lying about the backup lights.

I strode past her, wishing I could see the resentment in her face. Before reaching the corner, I turned. "You coming?"

"Where?"

"I'm walking you back to your room. You shouldn't be out here alone."

She folded her arms, her tone dangerous. "Yet it's okay for you. Because you're a big, tough Firebrand and all."

"You don't know enough about the people who work here, princess." It was no bluff. I'd looked up the profiles of every single neurotech worker I could find, trying to determine who Dane's missing spy had been, and discovered a few suspicious identities in the process. None were people I'd want Legacy meeting alone in a dark hallway. "If something happens to me, nobody will cry about it. But hey, if you want to wander around in the dark by yourself, be my guest."

She hesitated.

"Fine." I shrugged and started to walk away.

She trotted up behind me. "For the record, I'd rather be alone than surrounded by hundreds of people. It just . . . doesn't happen often for me."

There was a rare note of vulnerability in her voice. I tried not to act surprised. "Daddy a little overprotective?"

She snorted. I waited, hoping another expletive would escape her lips, but she said nothing more.

Silence filled the hallways around us for several minutes. As we approached the women's section of the wing, I spoke. "I'm surprised your dad let you come, with your Mom and all."

"He didn't have a choice."

"That's what this is about, then. Proving a point, showing your dad who's in charge. Hurting him like only a daughter can."

She halted. The darkness veiled her expression, but her voice was like a jagged diamond. "You know nothing about my life, Firebrand. Don't presume you do."

"Fates. I'm making conversation. I couldn't care less what you and your family do."

"I doubt that. You followed me here—"

"I did *not* follow you."

"—and then you followed me around the lab, waiting for the lights to turn off. Now you're prying for information. As if I would tell you anything."

I placed myself in her path, blocking her exit. "My being here has absolutely nothing to do with you. Okay?"

"Prove it."

"Fine. I need the money."

It had slipped out without my permission. I mentally kicked myself, unsure why I was bothered by the admission. It wasn't a lie, exactly. Maybe that was part of the problem.

Legacy looked taken aback. "That's it?"

"Yes. Money. It's this thing that ensures we can survive. Food, shelter, clothing, and the like. You wouldn't understand."

"I know more about it than you think."

I pinned her with a cold glare. "I doubt that."

"Look." She sighed. "As fun as it is to argue with you, I really just want to be left alone. Give me space, and I won't push you anymore. Assuming you give me the same respect."

"Done. No questions. Just do me a favor and don't wander the hallways late at night."

I expected a sharp retort, but the fight seemed to have left her. She watched me for a long moment. With more light, I knew her green eyes would be piercing my own. Reading, probing, digging into my soul like they had during our after-school conversation.

Her voice was quiet when she finally spoke. "I shouldn't wander at night because you want the hallways all to yourself or because you're the gallant type and you actually care?"

The question was genuine enough. I hesitated before responding. Her late-night explorations *would* complicate my mission here. Keeping my secrets was hard enough without a Hawking trying to pry into my life.

But at the core, I didn't want anything bad to happen to Legacy Hawking, either. It wasn't her fault Daddy Hawking refused to improve living conditions for a third of his citizens. For all I knew, she was a normal teenager trying to live a normal life away from a very abnormal family. In that way, we were alike.

As much as I tried to suppress it, the intrigue surfaced again. I'd spoken to her only three times and already knew what most people didn't. Legacy was a fascinating combination of confidence without cockiness, beauty without self-obsession, and unexpected wit. If our families weren't mortal enemies, I would have enjoyed an accidental night-time meeting or two.

I shifted my feet, bothered by the thought. "I'll let you wonder about that," I muttered and increased my pace.

She said nothing more.

———

MY ROOMMATE, Lars, was still up when I got back. Quiet kid, a little creepy. Probably a gamer considering how long he'd spent on the IM-NET today. We'd barely exchanged two words while dropping off our belongings earlier, which was exactly how I preferred it. Now he sat on his bed, one leg extended and staring at the wall with a dazed expression.

When I closed the door, his eyes focused and he straightened. "There you are."

I grabbed my bag, which I'd carelessly left on my bed, and tossed it underneath. The pockets were still secured, but that didn't mean they were untouched. A stupid mistake. "You don't need to wait up for me."

"I didn't. I'm used to staying up till three. Doesn't look like that will bother you." He raised an eyebrow at the bag I'd just dumped on the floor. "You aren't going to unpack?"

"No point." I only had two spare shirts and an extra pair of trousers, none of which would be needed with our fancy blue tech uniforms. I hadn't tried mine on yet. I had the rest of my life for that, thanks to good ol' Uncle Dane.

"Is it true you went to Legacy Hawking's school?"

I groaned inwardly. So much for keeping to himself. "Yup."

"You two friends?"

I snorted.

He leaned back against the wall. "That's right. You're from the Shadows. I'm surprised they let you in here at all with how paranoid Hawking is these days."

I grunted, hoping he'd take the hint, and removed my shoes. They were nearly worn through. I couldn't decide if Neuromen-issued shoes would be a relief or a nuisance.

"I bet Legacy's as clueless about real life as her dad. Did you see her wander off during the tour today? I thought the escort's head would blow right open."

"Tell me about you," I interrupted, ready to talk about anything *but* Legacy Hawking right now. "Where're you from, your family, all the usual questions."

He saw right through it. "You don't like talking about her. Interesting."

"There are plenty of other things to talk about. Things that actually matter." I plopped down on my bed. It was harder than Uncle Dane's mattress at home, but the bed frame was a nice change.

"You're a Firebrand then."

I scowled. If he'd dug that deep already, I definitely should have taken my duffel bag with me earlier. "Most from the Shadows are."

"Do you have the tattoo?"

No use lying. The guy would see it eventually. I pulled my T-shirt down, noting that the skin was still a fierce pink. "Got it last night."

"No way." He scrambled off his mattress to take a closer look. "A round flame?"

"The Undiscerning Sun. It's symbolic of the kind of country we want but don't have yet, a place where everyone has the same opportunity to excel."

Lars continued to stare. Definitely creepy. I released my shirt collar, letting the fabric fall over the sensitive skin once again.

He just looked thoughtful. "Is it that bad in the Shadows, then?"

"Worse. Housing is expensive. Jobs don't pay well, and since we're locked into our career of choice, bosses can treat their employees however they want. Something the Hawkings didn't think about when they set up their little utopia, and they aren't listening when we point out the problem." I shrugged. "But we're trying to change things peacefully."

"And if that doesn't work, you'll change them by force."

It wasn't a question I wanted to answer. I decided to let Lars think what he liked. "I'd appreciate it if you could keep all this quiet."

"Sure. I've actually considered taking the oath myself. I've always wanted to stun someone in real life." He lifted an invisible weapon and pretended to aim it at my chest.

We didn't give stunners to new recruits, but I didn't tell him so. "Any idea what's in store tomorrow? Sounds like there's testing the next few days."

"Yep. Full day of exams tomorrow, probably to make sure we're all qualified. Bet Legacy Hawking won't even make it past dinnertime. Can't wait to see Virgil make her a receptionist in a skanky little skirt."

Resentment gripped my chest at that, even though it was the type of joke I might have laughed at weeks ago. "You never know. She seems decently smart."

A smile tugged at his mouth. "What does that matter?"

I rolled my eyes, swiped some soap, and headed for the washroom. "The schedule said something about fitness testing."

"Day after tomorrow. Not sure why our physical fitness matters." He climbed back onto his bed. His irises turned a pale-pink color once more. Back to the game.

Relieved, I reviewed the week's schedule again before dismissing it. I wasn't worried about any of the exams, but being scheduled every minute of the day would make it hard to explore unnoticed. If Neuromen considered fitness a priority, maybe I could switch my daily running schedule to nighttime.

Maybe Legacy will be out again.

I shook my head, willing the unruly thought out of my head for good. Legacy was a distraction I didn't need, now or ever. Especially with my mother lying in a hospital bed, her fate unknown and entirely dependent upon how I spent my time here. I would discover what that implant update did. I would pass the information along to Dane and buy freedom for Mom and myself.

Just then, a message arrived from Ned Harris, Uncle Dane's alias. I opened it, froze, and deleted it immediately.

I'M WAITING.

NINE

LEGACY

I woke to the sound of whimpering. The clock read 05:16.

Rolling over, I found Millian lying still in her bed across the room. A faint glow beneath the door from the hallway's emergency lights was barely enough to find the outline of her face. It was scrunched in agony. Her black lashes fluttered against her dark cheeks.

I watched her, unsure what to do. Was she sick or just having a nightmare? If I woke her, she'd sooner attack me than thank me.

Slowly, I swung my legs over the mattress and leaned over to sweep the hair away from her wet cheeks. Not sweat but tears. She was crying in her sleep—a feat I'd once believed impossible until I'd experienced it for myself over the past year.

"Shh," I whispered. "It's okay."

Another whimper tore from her mouth, but her breathing had already begun to slow. A stab of guilt hit me about our conversation yesterday. I knew little about her other than her speech about taking Virgil's job someday. I'd been too irritated about my own accommodations to recognize that Millian might be just as uncomfortable with our new home.

I sorted through my implant files and pulled up an early capture of my parents when they were engaged at age twenty-six. Dad held Mom on his back, her head hanging back in delighted laughter, arms wrapped around his shoulders to keep from slipping off. It was informal, casual, and very much *not* Dad. Mom had a way of igniting joy in him.

Had people called her a science nerd too? Or had they seen her as smart, bursting with potential, and determined? Had Mom intended to take Virgil's job someday? To wrench the world into a better version of itself armed with pure science?

That was my problem, I realized. Jealousy. It wasn't that Millian had earned her place here, necessarily. It was that she knew who she was and what she wanted.

I was only here to chase the ghost of someone I loved— someone my roommate resembled more than myself.

Using the corner of her blanket, I gently wiped her cheeks. She mumbled in her sleep and rolled over, nightmare forgotten. In the dim green light coming from the hallway, something on the inner skin of her wrist caught my eye. Tiny scratches, like she'd fallen out of a tree or had a run-in with a feral cat. Except these scratches were too long and neat, like old railroad tracks. One looked darker than the others. A fresh wound. There had to be a razor blade hidden among her belongings.

My heart squeezed. As pulled together as she seemed, Millian was broken too. Maybe even more than I was.

Perhaps having her for a roommate wouldn't be so terrible after all.

I climbed back into bed, resolving to attempt a real conversation with Millian tomorrow. Then I pulled the blankets up to my chin and did something I hadn't done in a very long time. I allowed myself to remember.

MOM STILL WASN'T BACK from work when dinnertime came. Dad insisted we wait for her. She often walked in thirty or forty minutes late, apologizing that she'd lost track of time, her hair only half contained in its bun and a faraway look in her eyes. Dad always said we couldn't blame her for loving her work.

But that night was different.

Half an hour passed, then one hour, and finally two. I wasn't sure whether it was Alex's complaining or Dad's premonition that something was wrong that made him finally agree to let us eat without her. While Alex shoveled down his food, Dad and I picked at ours as we watched the door. I must have pulled up her location on the IM-NET a dozen times, watching her transport close the distance between work and home in an agonizingly slow manner.

We were nearly done when she walked in. Her bun was once again askew, but there was no brightness in her eyes tonight. Instead, she looked like a woman who'd lost someone she loved.

"What's wrong?" I asked, but Dad simply rose to his feet and wrapped her in his arms. They stood there like that for at least a minute. I remember how tightly his hand clung to her back, as if refusing to let her pull away. When she finally did, there was resignation in her face.

I left my light on that night. It was our code—it meant I wanted to talk with Mom about something. Without fail, she would creep in and sit on my bed, softly stroking my face to wake me if I had fallen asleep. Our talks often lasted an hour or longer. We discussed school, boys, even the aspects of work she was allowed to talk about. I invented questions I knew the answers to just to keep her there longer. Once I descended into soft slumber, she'd turn off the light and sneak out.

But that night, neither of us had much to say. I couldn't tell her about Derik the ex-boyfriend. She couldn't tell me what had kept her at work. After a moment of staring at everything in the room but each other, she'd asked a single question. I was too tired, too absorbed in my own day, and too troubled by her odd behavior to notice how her eyes clung to me as I formed a reply.

It wasn't the question, but my answer that haunted me most.

A buzzer sounded in my ear, tearing the offending memory away. The morning alarm.

The memory slipped away like mist. An unfamiliar ceiling greeted me as I forced my eyes open. Millian's bed was empty, blankets thrown askew. The sound of running water could be heard through the closed washroom door.

I rubbed the sleep from my eyes. Last night's trip to the garden had yielded nothing new. It was like the graffiti had never existed, nor the blood on the floor. Nothing but the clean white Virgil preferred. Then my exploring had resulted in an uncomfortable conversation with a Firebrand rather than answers. All I knew was that some kind of cover-up had occurred. If there was a link to Mom's death, I had to find it.

Three facts remained. First, Mom had gone to work the next day and never returned. Second, I hadn't stopped her.

Third, I *should* have stopped her.

The worst part were the lies my heart whispered, like solving the mystery about Mom's death meant that I would find her at last. That I could bring her home and everything would be normal again. That she would forgive me for my carelessness and we could all move on as a family.

My brain inevitably pulled me down to reality. It was like Alex had said. Mom was gone and wasn't coming back.

At the corner of my swimming vision, the day's schedule icon appeared. I wiped my eyes on a sleeve and steeled myself for what lay ahead.

My first day of testing had begun.

TEN
LEGACY

Later that morning, I sat back in my chair, dismissing the exam screen with three quick blinks. Done. I'd recognized terms here and there, but the questions hadn't made much sense. Frustration solidified in my stomach. If anyone doubted I belonged here, today's results would clinch it. My understanding of basic science was average, but nobody else in this room fit that description. Was there a position even lower than lab assistant?

If only I'd thought to brush up on my physics.

Across the room, Millian scowled as she finished and dismissed the display on her eye screen. Her expression gave me a twinge of hope. Maybe it was difficult for everyone.

Kole was the only other person in the room who'd finished early. He sat, too relaxed, looking around the room and examining every face as if looking for something. His eyes drifted right over me like I was a stranger.

Good. I had no desire to befriend a Firebrand no matter how good he looked in his dark-blue Neuromen uniform. He adjusted his collar as if uncomfortable. Was it because he now wore a new sun tattoo under the golden stripe across his chest?

The last boy stirred a few minutes later, the pink in his eyes fading away. Done.

A second later, Soren entered wearing the same tight bun and stern expression as yesterday. "Thank you. You may return to the cafeteria for lunch, followed by another round of testing at 14:00. You may visit the common rooms or walk the grounds before then, but please stay out of the lab wing. Our scientists have set their usual priorities aside to sort your test results today. Your standings will be posted later." She left the second she finished talking.

I checked the time. Nearly two hours to spare. Perfect.

I stopped by the garden on the way to the lab wing, hoping I'd missed something in the dark last night. The wall and floor were as clean as ever. Hopefully the labs held a new clue.

A blinking light caught my attention as I turned to leave —a ceiling camera, trained directly on the graffiti wall. Had they installed the camera long ago and the artist hadn't noticed? Or was its installation in response to the event, an attempt to discourage the artist from repeating the deed?

I recalled yesterday's bloodstain and grimaced. Whoever the artist was, they wouldn't be returning anytime soon.

Mom's lab was locked tight when I arrived.

I'd been in this wing before, two years earlier, on a family visitation day. Mom had been her usual calm self, but she couldn't hide the light in her eyes. She was proud of her work. I remembered bouncing on my toes in anticipation of seeing her mysterious project as she unlocked the door. But when the door opened, there was nothing to see.

No trace of anything interesting. Just a regular lab with an oversized steel table and a desk in the corner.

"It isn't ready yet," she'd explained, giving me a wink. "I'll show it to you someday. I just have to work out some issues first."

She'd never said what "it" was, and Dad wouldn't answer my questions. It wasn't his place, he said. I suspected her silence also had something to do with her contract. If this experiment was as groundbreaking as she made it seem, they wouldn't want anyone to discover it until the right moment.

That moment never came. The explosion had taken both Mom and her experiment away forever.

I leaned back against the door for support and drew a deep, slow breath. Standing here, so close to the place she'd spent her last moments, made the pain return tenfold. This was a bad idea. The fire had taken everything with it, along with most of the lab wing. All this had been recently rebuilt. My knees trembled, struggling to keep me upright.

Maybe it was better that the door was locked. I obviously wasn't ready. I gave the door one last look and turned to go.

"Miss Hawking," a deep voice said, making me jump. "I've just given you access. Draw closer to the door, and it should open."

I looked around, breath suspended in my chest. No cameras, no speakers. That meant . . . someone had *talked* to me through my implant. Not just anyone, either. Director Virgil. How long had he been watching me stand here, fighting off my memories? And how had he hacked into my implant speakers?

Feeling my cheeks warm, I moved closer. Half a second

later, there was a loud click and the door nudged open. The moment I stepped inside, the inside lights came on.

"Make yourself at home. I'll be in shortly." A tiny click, and he was gone.

I shuddered. This couldn't be legal. Surely Director Virgil was breaking all kinds of privacy laws by hacking into my brain. Besides that tiny click, there'd been no warning whatsoever. He could have listened to every conversation I'd had today.

The warmth in my cheeks was something else now. Dad would hear about this. Well, when he was ready to speak to me again.

In the meantime, I took in my surroundings. The lab looked exactly as it had before, identical to every other room here. White, boring, blah. The far window's brilliant blue reflecting the outside bay was the only color—real glass, not the green-tinted safety kind. The usual table stood in the room's center, though it looked smaller in scale than Mom's. The only differences were a fire extinguisher bracketed to the wall and the ceiling sprinklers. I didn't exactly blame Virgil for the new safety obsession.

There was also no bag hanging from the hook near the door. I'd given her that bag for her birthday. We'd never see it again.

I leaned against the wall, drawing in a series of long, slow breaths to control the emotions churning inside me and grateful I hadn't eaten lunch yet.

Mom thought in numbers, explained things using properties and atoms, and felt most at home in her crisp, blue uniform. I could almost sense her here, like a presence in the darkness only I could feel. I imagined her standing at that table, taking notes while hunched over a jumble of chemicals, her too-large goggles slipping down her petite nose and making her eyes look huge.

Her safety goggles hadn't done much to protect her that day.

It was Dad who'd come to school to tell me. I could still see every inch of the officiator's office, how my chest felt like it had exploded right along with the lab. This lab.

"You were the lab's leading scientist," I said, my voice stabbing the silence. "You should have been more careful." The room didn't answer.

Footsteps in the hallway.

I turned just in time to see Director Virgil open the door. He looked as disheveled as when I'd seen him a year ago. His gray eyebrows were messy and round, hovering over his eyes like two overgrown bushes. It made his balding head look even more strange gleaming in the bright lights overhead. Only a ring of hair remained, extending from ear to ear.

"I hoped you'd find this place." He gestured to the room. "We finished rebuilding this part of the wing just last month. I think we got it right. What do you think?"

I ignored the question. "How did you talk to me just now?"

His eyebrows lifted in surprise. "Ah. I bet that was startling. I sometimes forget that our newest candidates have never experienced that before. Our security protocols get triggered when a person's implant location breeches a protected area, which enables us to communicate with the trespasser in an audible manner temporarily. Now, since it's obvious this lab is of interest to you, and in memory of your mother, I've issued a permanent implant authorization that allows you to come and go as you please. Any other candidate arriving at this door will receive a warning to return to their authorized wing."

I eyed him. "Thank you, but that doesn't answer my question. How exactly did you hack into my internal speakers?"

"I wouldn't call it 'hacking,' exactly. All implants had the ability to deliver emergency messages from the beginning. It was initially intended for children who can't read, as a security precaution. But your father believed internal audio messages raised privacy concerns, so he made it illegal. Now all messages are delivered with text unless the user authorizes a call."

A decision I agreed with. "Then why use it here?"

"Private company. Upon signing the contract yesterday, you authorized your implant to be monitored. But don't worry. We aren't allowed to view a person's implant feed visually, for example, nor see their personal files. The ability to speak to you was only activated once you entered this protected area. When you return to the graduate wing, that ability will be automatically blocked once again."

His face looked genuine, but my gut still crawled. "I think my dad should know about this anyway."

"He does. You should also know that the policy wasn't initiated here until after your mother died. Believe me, I wish I'd implemented it sooner. If I'd kept a closer watch on her, perhaps she'd still be with us." He motioned to the room. "This lab will remain empty for an entire year in memory of your mother. Enjoy it. It's my greatest desire that you feel at home here."

Somehow I doubted it was his *greatest* desire. "All due respect, sir, I can't feel at home if I'm worried about being spied on."

The briefest of pauses. "Here, I can promise you

privacy. If you wander into other unauthorized wings, you'll be subject to the same security as the others. Your father would never forgive me if something happened to you while under my care."

That much was true, I grudgingly admitted. Dad would never forgive Virgil for last year's explosion. The man was already fighting to keep his lab afloat. He wouldn't risk losing another Hawking and giving my father ammunition, privacy issues or not.

I filed the information away, determined to pick it apart later. For now, I had Director Virgil exactly where I wanted him. "I need to know exactly what happened that night. You didn't tell us much."

The director let his gaze sweep the room, taking in its contents like a fellow observer. "We still know less than I'd like. If only Andreah had come to me for help. I would have supplied her with the test subjects she needed. She must have been so confident in her experiment she downloaded the update herself to see if it worked. It didn't."

I stared at him. He hadn't told us this part before. Everyone made it sound like it was some freak chemical accident.

"But wait," I said, still trying to piece it together. "How can a neurotech experiment create an explosion big enough to topple half a wing? It involves wires and electrodes, not explosives."

He turned to face me, his expression sad. "That question has kept me up many nights since. We found no residue of explosive chemicals or powders and no manual detonation devices. Even our best experts have been unable to determine the cause."

I examined him for a long time, but there was truth in

the man's eyes. He seemed almost as frustrated with the lack of answers as I was.

"She obviously believed in her research, and that's all we need to know." He placed a hand on my shoulder and squeezed it. "I'm truly sorry. If it's any comfort, we've revamped security tenfold since then. Nothing like that will ever happen again."

I just nodded.

He hesitated. "There's something else we need to discuss, Miss Hawking. It's something of a delicate matter."

"More delicate than a scientist blowing herself up?" I asked bitterly.

He looked up at the ceiling as if reconsidering, then leveled his gaze at me. "I can't tell you how pleased we were that you accepted the invitation to come. Truly. It was a pleasant surprise, and we look forward to mending any resentment between myself and your honored family."

Translation: He hadn't really wanted me to come.

"I suppose I wanted something different from life," I said carefully, unsure where this was going.

"A familiar cause. My parents wanted me to become a plumber. Obviously, I chose a different path, just as you have. I can imagine your father wasn't too pleased. It must have been hard to go against his wishes for your future."

"Not really." A lie, but this man didn't deserve the truth.

"I see." His fatherly act slipped, the irritation behind his words evident. "Well, you're an adult now, so let me speak frankly. The press coverage surrounding your Declaration was remarkable. We've received several rather generous donations since you arrived. The public's eye is upon you, Miss Hawking. They want you to succeed. The problem is, your test results today were far from promising."

I stiffened. It was clear where this conversation was headed.

"Your talents may lie in other areas. Public relations, for one. I have a proposal for you in that regard. But if you'd prefer to remain in the scientific track, you're welcome to take the test again."

I wanted to laugh at that. The meaning was clear—this was no simple proposal. It was pure and undefiled black-mail. Reject his offer and I would be demoted and slandered to the press before I learned anything about Mom and her disaster of a project. Director Virgil pretended to be a compassionate man, but I couldn't forget for a moment who he was. "I'm listening."

"We're holding a broadcast announcement regarding our latest update. It will be remarkably unlike previous updates, and we are rather proud of it. I'd like you to be the one to announce it to the world."

I frowned. *More cameras.* "Broadcasts aren't exactly my thing."

"Your script will be written for you. All you have to do is read the words aloud. Since this announcement is intended for the general public, there will be little science involved. We'll give you an office and the position permanently. You can spend the rest of your life away from your more scientifically-inclined peers in the other wings."

I imagined a life of forced isolation and grimaced. I didn't have many friends, true, but that didn't mean I had no desire to make them. Besides, I hadn't come here to spend my life in an office, especially if it meant limited access to the rest of the building. "What if I prefer to finish Training Week before I decide?"

He looked surprised at the request. "Agree to make this announcement, and I suppose we could allow you to attend

Training Week as if nothing has changed. I'll ensure your results hover somewhere in the middle of the standings to avoid angering the press. At the end of the week, however, I'll need a decision. Your results will have to change drastically by then if you want to make lab assistant."

My temples throbbed with the beginning of a headache. I had no desire to play his games right now. "When is the announcement?"

"Three days from today. You'll be among the first to boast involvement with this exciting project. I'm sure your father will be very proud." Another patronizing smile.

Right. The father who wasn't likely to check in anytime soon. "I want to see the speech beforehand."

"I'll send it the night before so you can practice. I know you distrust me, Miss Hawking, but you and I want the same thing. We value our freedom. This isn't the type of decision I usually offer candidates."

My frown deepened at that. Was this freedom? Because it sure didn't feel like it. Kole had once called it exchanging one prison for another. And this man—my mom's former boss—held the key.

I'm a Hawking, and I will do what's required. If reading some stupid script was the cost of solving Mom's mystery, I didn't have much choice.

"Fine. I'm in."

"Excellent." He inclined his head and hurried for the door. Then he turned back to me. "You may not see your place in the world yet, Miss Hawking, but I do. Your future will be a grand one."

ELEVEN

KOLE

THE NEXT DAY was the first I enjoyed since my arrival. Fitness testing day.

We spent the morning lifting weights and stretching in the lab's private gym, a section of rooms with high ceilings and harsh lighting. Why these people cared how far over my toes I could reach was beyond me, but it was such a relief after yesterday's exams, I didn't care.

The day's events also meant new workout uniforms—a loose black shirt with the usual gold stripe across the chest, a pair of soft shorts, and lab-issued running shoes that weren't half bad.

Finally, the judges arrived for our assigned aerobic testing. They began calling graduates over to the track. I continued my stretches, itching to finally get my running rhythm going again.

A man with an enormous forehead and even larger double chin called my name. I trotted out and listened to his instructions. A quick warm-up and then a series of sprints. They'd receive all the information they needed from my implant readings.

I frowned at that. "Don't you need my permission to look those up?"

He just smirked. "No."

Right. The contract. I shook my head, headed to the track's inner lane, and started off at a slow jog.

Minutes later, I found my stride. The sprints Forehead Guy had asked for grew progressively longer and closer together, but I found myself smiling each time I passed him. Maybe my stay here wouldn't be so mind-numbing after all.

I reached the finish line of the final sprint, but instead of motioning me over, the proctor waved me on. "Two more laps, 80 percent speed!"

Distance, then. Finally, my kind of workout. I shot him a thumbs-up and focused on breathing and regulating my stride. Dane could make demands of my time, but this—this was the one thing that truly belonged to me.

Footsteps pounded behind me to the right. I looked over my shoulder to see Legacy Hawking running in the second lane. Her eyes met mine and held them for several seconds. Then a mischievous smile crossed her face. I knew exactly what it meant.

The race had begun.

I increased my speed just as she did. After a minute, my lungs demanded more air, and I obliged, keeping my breaths even. No Hawking would hear me panting.

She remained at my flank, but I sensed that was to conserve energy and not from a lack of speed. In fact, our pace matched nearly stride for stride. If she wanted the inside, she'd have to fall back and run behind me. I felt a glimmer of satisfaction at the thought of this particular girl staring helplessly at my back.

When we reached the straightaway, something caught

fire inside Legacy because she dug in and started gaining ground. She ran right beside me now, her expression incredibly focused, eyes narrowed in determination. Every inch of her body propelled her forward. She had almost perfect form and barely looked winded.

I refused to be impressed. The Hawkings likely had personal trainers on salary. She would have a gym much like this in her house. This was nothing but a daily workout for her.

Her eyes flicked to mine and held them once again. Then she winked.

Oh, it was on.

My chest burned now, but I stubbornly pushed the pain to the back of my mind. I would not lose to Legacy Hawking.

I managed to hold a slight lead around the turn, but we were stride for stride at the straightaway. My proctor stepped forward and shouted, "One more lap!" as I passed.

This was a faster pace than I usually ran. It wasn't exactly conducive to sidewalk exercise. I'd sprinted around town a few times at night, but that required slowing around corners to watch for speeding transports.

To my relief, Legacy's breathing grew more labored around the first turn. Finally. I imagined her drifting to the outside and halting for a break, feigning some kind of injury. Or better yet, praising me as the victor.

She suddenly fell back.

I looked over my right shoulder to make sure she was okay. Big mistake. The next second, she reappeared to my left. She'd dodged behind me to take the inside and shorter route.

I wanted to be angry, but my exhausted mind was too

fixated on how powerful her strides were as we reached the back straightaway. There was something far too captivating about the flush in her cheeks and the way her eyes shone, her long dark ponytail swinging behind her.

I shook my head to clear it. Obviously my brain needed more oxygen.

As we rounded the back turn, a shout arose from the waiting candidates. They'd seen the battle and taken sides.

"Go, Shadows!" a girl called as we passed.

A voice I recognized as Lars's shouted a suggestive comment at Legacy. She pressed her lips together, the only indication she'd heard. Imagining how it would feel to plant a fist in my roommate's face fueled another burst of speed, and I drew even with her once more.

My proctor stepped onto the track, signaling me to stop. But Legacy didn't slow down as we crossed the finish line and rounded into another turn. We weren't done yet.

This was a record-breaking time for me. I knew it in my burning thighs and gasping breaths. Never before had I sprinted at top speed for so long. Legacy's cheeks, now a furious red, betrayed the same. This was no longer about skill and practice. There would be a victor and a loser, and neither of us were okay with the latter—Legacy because victory was her birthright, and I because losing was mine.

The thought shot me forward by half a stride. I threw my entire body into every movement, imagining myself a blade parting the very air itself. Legacy growled. Like a wild animal, she lunged forward to overtake the lost distance and plunged into an entirely new level of speed.

We reached the last turn. My chest felt ready to shut down, the air I so desperately needed refusing to enter my lungs. Black claws crept along the edges of my vision. The shouting of our audience swelled until I couldn't distinguish one voice from another.

Legacy was a full stride ahead now, barely within arm's reach. I wouldn't catch her. Not because she was faster but because she was simply fresher. It wasn't a fair contest. Nothing about our comparative lives was fair.

There was only one thing left to do.

I cried out. She fell for it, looking over her right shoulder in alarm. She *did* care.

I took the moment to reclaim the inside and charged for the straightaway before she realized she'd been duped at her own game. A deep laugh broke from her throat.

Our proctors scrambled back as we approached the finish line, clearing the track. They looked positively baffled at this development.

Legacy's laughter only increased as I flew over the line first. I gasped for breath and slowed, finally looking behind me to see what was so funny. The heiress stood bent over, chest heaving, and laughing so hard she seemed positively out of her mind.

At my expression, she bowled over and threw herself onto the ground, her laughter an odd mixture of giggling and gulping air.

"That . . . was . . . fun," she managed between gasps.

My legs shook so badly I wondered if I'd join her. Instead, I walked over and offered a hand, still panting. "Good race."

Before I knew what was happening, she'd hooked her leg around mine and brought me down.

Dane's training kicked in, and I landed lightly, rolling away. Standing was a little harder. My legs had chosen now to betray me. Every other recruit in the gym ran over from the warm-up area, all smiles and congratulations.

"That was amazing, man," Lars said, clapping me on the back, although his gaze was on Legacy. She still lay laughing on the track, one knee bent. Her shirt clung to her body, revealing more of her curves than usual and drawing every pair of male eyes in the room. Even the proctors', I noticed with a frown.

"That was stupid," Millian muttered, pulling Legacy to her feet. "What were you guys trying to prove? That you could make yourselves sick before dinnertime?"

That set Legacy laughing again. Her usual scowls were completely absent, replaced with an untethered joy that seemed so unlike her, so un-Hawking-like I fought to hide a grin. Her bright green held a new light, a shining contrast to her flushed face. She stood and brushed a stray hair back toward her ponytail before placing a hand on her hip, her chest still rising and falling in time with mine.

As oxygen returned to my brain, the thrill of victory was replaced with shame. Millian was right. Fun as it was, that race was the dumbest thing I could have done today. Now everyone's eyes were on us. *Together.* They'd assume our competition meant more than it did.

Legacy sobered as well. Maybe she was remembering my declaration that we weren't friends. An early attempt to send a strong message, contradicted by this first test of determination.

I couldn't make that mistake again.

Legacy's cheeks were bright red now, but it wasn't from exertion. "Not bad for a . . . Shadows guy."

We both knew what she'd been about to say. The fact that she'd avoided outing me in front of our entire recruiting class and two proctors meant something, but I wasn't sure what.

"Hey, show-off," Forehead Guy said, tearing my attention from Legacy. "You aren't finished yet. Come cool down with some more stretches, or I'll take points off your standings."

"They both need some serious cooling down," muttered the girl who'd cheered me on.

I felt Legacy's eyes on my back as I walked away.

TWELVE

LEGACY

"Yes, I know who you are, and I still think you should be in bed." The worker stubbornly folded her arms, keeping her wheeled waste bin within reach. She wore her hair short, like a young boy's, giving her a youthful look despite the gray strands in her hair. I remembered her from the first day. She'd given me a smile and a wink. There would be no such kindness today.

I sighed inwardly. To say my interviewing attempts were going poorly was an understatement. This was the fourth worker I'd cornered tonight, and she seemed even less willing to help than the others.

"I only have a few questions. If it helps, I'll . . . I'll clean with you."

She snickered. "You? Hawking's daughter?"

"I will. If you'll answer my questions, that is."

The woman gave me a skeptical look. "You ever mopped a floor before?"

"Of course." I couldn't think of a specific instance, but surely I'd done it once or twice. "My mother worked here for twenty years. I'm wondering if you knew her."

She shoved a mop into my hands and motioned to the dirty water in the bucket next to the waste bin. I wrinkled my nose. Neuromen created the most advanced technology in the country, yet this poor woman was forced to scrub floors like some medieval maidservant.

The worker folded her arms again, watching me carefully. She didn't mean for me to work alongside her. She wanted me to do it *for* her.

Cringing, I plunged the mop into the water and splattered it onto the floor. Then I began to scrub. The mop was heavier than it looked.

The woman looked amused, but her expression faded quickly. "Doctor Hawking was a good soul. So kind to me and the others."

I nodded. "She was kind to everyone."

"That she was. Volunteered to participate in her last experiment, I did."

I nearly dropped the mop. "Really?"

"That's what I said."

But that didn't make sense. According to Virgil, Mom had attempted the update on herself before the project even went to human trials. "What did she have you doing?"

She looked surprised. "You don't know? She programmed our implants with something new. Or at least she was supposed to. Mine didn't work."

I frowned. "It didn't work, or you didn't notice a difference?"

"Not sure. All I know is that some people didn't like it, and she tried to reverse it, but that didn't work either. Director Virgil sent them all off for treatment and I haven't seen them since. Your mama was pretty upset."

The information came faster than I could process it. "So the update didn't work for you, and that was a good thing?"

"Maybe, maybe not. They're free, and I'm still here."

I wasn't sure whether she meant the test subjects were released from Virgil's service or dead. I didn't dare ask. "Then Mom's update backfired, and she was sad about it."

"Very. Kind woman, your mother. Scrubbed her lab spotless before she left every night so I wouldn't have to. You missed a spot by the corner."

I followed her gaze to a dirt stain and attacked it. This was definitely harder than it looked. "You said Virgil sent those test subjects away, but he swears he didn't know anything about the project until after the explosion."

The woman snickered. "He swears a lot of things. The question you should be asking is why Virgil didn't conduct an investigation afterward."

The mop froze in my hands. "He didn't?"

"Nope. Just cleared the rubble and rebuilt, all hush-hush. Expected them to come looking for me and anyone else involved, but they didn't question nobody."

I let that sink in. Hadn't Virgil mentioned bringing experts in to detect explosives and chemicals? Either he or this woman was lying, and I couldn't think of a single reason why the janitor would mislead me about this.

Mom always said that lies were like ants—a single one meant hundreds of others lurked out of sight.

I should have been excited to get my first real lead, but all I felt was a sinking sensation in my stomach. Publicly, Virgil had blamed the explosion on Mom's negligence. It was his lies that had ignited the slander and gossip about my family over the past year. He'd lied *to my face*.

My grip on the mop was so tight I could have snapped it in two. "There's a white wall in the garden with a camera trained on it. Is it significant?"

"I'd say so. Used to be Virgil's office before they built

the new wing. It's sealed off now. Put the camera on it because some fool tried to get in there a few weeks ago, but it's been empty for years. Even if he succeeded, he would've been disappointed."

So much for that lead. "Last question. Do you know what caused my mom's explosion?"

She hesitated, then shook her head. "Nothing related to her project, I imagine. Wasn't a flammable thing in sight. No chemicals, no powder. Still can't figure out how it happened. And I think we're done here."

I looked down at the floor. A centimeter of dirty water covered the once-white floor, turning it a sickly gray. "Sorry. I'm not very experienced."

"Didn't expect you to be. Just wanted to see if you'd do it. But we're done because you've already stayed too long." She gestured to a distant light blinking down the hall. A camera.

I'd nearly forgotten. "Thank you."

"Your mama was a good woman. That's the only reason I agreed to this conversation. Be smart, all right? Not all of them can be trusted." She yanked the mop from me, and with a practiced hand began to soak up the puddle of dirty water I'd spread around the shiny white floor.

———

THE WOMAN'S words consumed my thoughts on my way back to the dorms.

That angry inner core burned bright with a red heat. I'd been right to come. Mom's death grew more suspicious all the time. But if her death wasn't related to the project itself, what was the cause? If Virgil was behind it, why stage a violent explosion that destroyed a huge chunk of his own enterprise? Dad had said the reconstruction alone had nearly put them under financially, not to mention the resulting months of lost work.

Distant laughter pulled me up short. The power restriction hadn't taken effect yet. By the sound of things, the candidates' common area was full tonight.

Curious, I made my way to the door and peered in. The lounge boasted a long table, a dozen haphazardly scattered chairs, and four sofas over which several recruits were draped. A couple embraced in the corner, oblivious to the laughter and chatter around them. Millian sat on one of the sofas. Her hands moved animatedly as she talked to another girl.

It stung that she hadn't invited me along. I tried to remind myself that I didn't care, that I'd pushed her and everyone else away for a reason. But it still hurt.

"The princess has arrived," an unfamiliar girl said with a smirk. She wore her dark hair in two thick braids. "Thought you'd be sleeping off your cute little race this afternoon."

I caught sight of Kole. He sat on the farthest sofa from the door, arms sprawled across the back of the sofa. A girl perched at his side. She could easily be a model with her long reddish-brown hair and tiny figure. She wore an easy smile and shiny lip gloss to go with it. She leaned over to say something close to his ear. Kole laughed in response. When he caught my gaze, the laughter stopped and he quickly looked away.

"He doesn't seem tired, though," the girl continued, still blocking my entrance. "Gotta love a guy with endurance. Is that sweat on your shirt, or did you spill your dinner?"

I looked down to find a dirty wet spot on my T-shirt. I'd managed to mop myself along with the floor.

Millian appeared at my side before I could answer. "Hey, I know you. Aren't you the one who keeps getting demoted? Zen or something?"

"Zen-NAY," Zenye corrected. "And I've been held back because of health problems. Not that it's any of your business."

"And my roommate isn't any of yours, so you can leave her alone." Millian took my arm and pulled me inside before I could react.

I tried to hide my surprise. "Thanks."

"Don't get any ideas. This doesn't mean I like you or anything. It just means I dislike her more. I can't stand fake, and she's as fake as it gets." Her grin softened the words.

I found myself smiling back. We had that in common, at least. "Why didn't you tell me about this get-together?"

"You disappeared. Where did you go, anyway?"

"Oh. I was . . . walking around."

Kole's eyes flicked to me again, then back to the redhead like they'd never left her.

Millian followed my gaze and pressed her lips together in disapproval. "I'd avoid that one if I were you. He keeps staring when you aren't looking. Oh, and stay away from that creepy guy in the corner too. I've heard things. Everyone else is decent, from what I can tell."

"So we just stand around and . . . talk?"

She coughed to cover a laugh. "You look terrified. Is your social anxiety that bad?"

I was used to parties and fake conversation, but this wasn't a political reception at the Block. This was real life. No guards, no cameras. Just kids my age living normal life as I'd never known it. "It's not that. I've just never done this before."

"Well, get used to it, because this is officially your new

social life. Go pick somebody and talk to them. Simple." She crossed the room to chat with a boy whose medium-brown features reminded me of Alex. He slouched when she arrived, his eyes darting around. I wasn't the only one who found this get-together baffling.

I swept the room. Everyone was already engaged in conversation except the corner guy Millian had mentioned. He looked up at my gaze, grinned, and stood.

Oops.

He made his way over and placed himself close enough that I took a step backward. "Hi."

His pale eyes reminded me distinctly of Derik. It made me shiver, but I managed to hide the emotion. "I'm Legacy."

"I know."

Eye roll. "Human beings usually have a name bestowed on them at birth. Unless you're telling me you're an exception."

He stared at me, something unsettling in his gaze. "Thanks for the education, princess."

"I could just look up your name, you know."

"But you won't because names don't matter. Only simple-minded people care about such things. We both want something different from the conversation, don't we?" He looked me up and down in a way that made me take another step back.

"I want nothing from this conversation, to be honest." Creepy guy, indeed. I looked around the room for a distraction, but there was none.

"I watched your boyfriend's little broadcast last year. He said you've experienced all kinds of things."

My chest seized. I had no desire to discuss what Derik had said about me. "*Ex*-boyfriend, and this conversation is done. I'll see you around."

I tried to step around him, but he blocked my escape. "Don't deny it. We both know you aren't as innocent as you pretend to be."

"Leave me alone," I hissed and pushed past him toward the door. The room swayed, my thoughts a raging fire.

This was why I didn't attend parties. It was also why I didn't have friends, and it was most certainly why I didn't have boyfriends anymore. *Stupid, stupid.*

I wasn't normal, nor would I ever be. Hadn't years of public school already taught me that much? I had just a few days to crack the mystery of Mom's death before I ended up alone in some dumb office, just like the fates had always decreed. I had to stay focused and stop dreaming about belonging anywhere else. I was a Hawking. I would do what was required, no matter how hard it hurt.

I turned my back on the group and left.

THIRTEEN
KOLE

I WATCHED Legacy storm out in anger. She'd been gone less than five seconds before Lars reclaimed his chair in the corner and returned to whatever game he'd been playing. His expression was that of nonchalance, but I noted the tightness in his shoulders.

"Are you in there?" The redhead sitting practically in my lap waved her hand in my face.

I resisted the urge to snap at her and tried to smile. "Yeah, sorry. I think my roommate just got rejected. I'd better go talk to him. Excuse me."

She actually stuck her lip out and pouted as I rose to my feet. I exhaled and crossed the room to Lars. "What did you say to her?"

He shot a dirty look at the doorway. "Doesn't matter."

"She looked upset. I think it matters."

"And you care because . . . ?"

"We aren't kids anymore. We're all coworkers advancing in our careers. Every person in this room deserves respect, even Legacy."

Lars slowly stood and got right in my face. "Interesting that you're lecturing me right now, roomie."

"Just don't be a jackass and we're good."

"And stay away from her, right? Because she's yours even though you won't make a move on her."

"Legacy Hawking belongs to nobody, least of all me. You'll be disappointed if you think she's here looking for love." The thought of Lars being a candidate for love at all angered me more than the expression on Legacy's face as she'd left, though I didn't dare consider why.

He snorted. "Nobody here is looking for *love*. You think that redhead over there cares where you stand on political issues or what your favorite transport model is? She just thought you were hot during your run this afternoon. That's it."

"Lars, I mean it. Stay away from Legacy."

"Or what, you'll strangle me in my sleep?" He stepped forward, forcing me to retreat a few centimeters. "I wonder if anyone here even knows you're a Firebrand. It might change Redhead's opinion of you if she knew. Maybe we should find out."

"Hey, Lars," said a girl with two thick braids over her shoulder, stopping at my side. "Some of the guys are having a Mars tournament. They heard you're a decent player and invited you to join in. That is, if you have the cash." She nodded toward a group congregating near the door.

Lars scowled. I doubted he had much cash at all, but the girl had read him correctly. "I've already beaten all my friends, but I'll come if they're up to the challenge."

The girl's eyes widened in mock worship. "I'm sure that will be something to watch."

Lars leaned in to stab me in the chest with his finger. "Mind your own business from now on."

"Same to you."

His gait had more swagger than usual as he joined the others, likely for this girl's benefit.

"You're welcome," she told me with a hint of a smile. "I'm Zenye. You and I have something important to discuss."

"Oh?"

"I know Ned Harris sent you. More importantly, I know why."

I stared at her. Only Firebrands knew Dane's alias. I should have known I wouldn't be the only spy here. My uncle didn't trust me enough for that. "Are you after the same information?"

"Nah, I already know all the answers. And no, I'm not telling you or Ned, so don't ask. I never took the oath." She pulled her collar back, exposing an expanse of clean skin across her collarbone. "You could say I'm simply a mercenary with a special interest in helping you accomplish your mission here."

"So Ned didn't send you."

"He asked me to help you. I agreed at a price he was willing to pay. Now, here's the problem—your hotheaded roommate over there is right. Your group's obsession with branding followers is dramatic and all, but it could cost you. The moment everyone here discovers your Firebrand connections, security will flag you for extra observation. Virgil won't allow you near the lab wing until your neurotech training is complete."

Which would take years. I didn't even have weeks. "Lars isn't serious. He wouldn't tell anyone."

"Guys do stupid things when girls are involved. However, if we alter your public records to contradict him, it will be your word against his. Anyone who wants to know can pull up your squeaky-clean implant records, see you're a good boy, and dismiss your roomie's accusations as false. Unless, of course, you shed that shirt of yours for some girl. Then I can't help you."

It took a second for the meaning of her words to sink in. Then I did a quick search for proximity records. My implant found her immediately. Zenye Holmes, age twenty-one. Everything looked normal except for one thing.

The parent fields read "Unknown."

That was impossible. New NORA had no true orphans. Each adopted child's records contained their new parents' names or at least the name of a guardian. Nobody was a true unknown.

I frowned. "If that can be done, why didn't Ned clear my record before I even arrived?"

"Record cleansing can only occur at a relay station. All the ones in town are run by stuffy-heads loyal to Hawking. But where I work, we can delete or change anything you want. You can rename yourself Unicorn Rainbow Falcon-face for all I care. But it isn't cheap. Every job I take on is a huge risk."

"I thought Dane was paying you."

"*Ned* paid me to keep an eye on you. You're paying me to change your identity. There's a difference."

Of course Dane would insist I pay for it myself. The cage felt like it was closing in. "I don't have much money."

"Sure you do. Just because it's in Mommy's medical savings account doesn't mean you can't reroute it."

My insides went cold. Not only had Zenye hacked into my financial accounts, she also knew about Mom. How far into my past had she researched? Because if she went deep enough . . .

I swallowed. Hard.

"I'm no criminal," she continued. "I don't intend to take all of it. I'd say fifty thousand credits ought to do it."

Now I choked. *"Fifty thousand?"* That was 80 percent of what I had saved for Mom's next medical bill. If I failed to make the payment, they would unplug Mom for good.

"This is about more than protecting your identity. You won't get the answers you want without me. There's something I need to show you, something you and your uncle will be very glad to discover."

Frustration welled up inside me. If I rejected her, the chances of my succeeding here were remote. If I accepted, Mom's life could be in danger in a different way. But if I found Dane's answers quickly enough, maybe he would help replenish the fund. Probably not, but maybe.

"Ten thousand," I said. "Paid *after* I get the answers I want."

Her black eyes glittered. "Forty, paid up front."

"Twenty upon satisfactory completion of my demands. My records get changed, and you show me what the new update does in detail." *Then I figure out a way to get Mom far away from Dane.*

"Twenty-five and done. Meet me in the garden at 15:00 tomorrow." She swept a braid back over her shoulder and sauntered away in much the same manner Lars had, except with more hips. Legacy didn't do that.

I gritted my teeth. *Stop it.* I was here to discover Virgil's secrets. I had to stop caring about Legacy and Lars and anything else distracting me from my true purpose. Mom's safety was more important than any of that, and I was closer to grasping it than ever.

I pulled up one last proximity record: Lars Druher. He hailed from one of the more wealthy districts. Clean record and high grades. But how much of that was really true?

Zenye's revelation had shifted my entire world. If Neuromen workers were truly running a black operation with public information, what did I really know about the people around me?

This explained why Dane cared so much about the implant update. With the power to alter records, he could wreak havoc on the Hawkings' orderly government system. Every citizen in the nation would be clamoring for new leadership after such confusion. The havoc it could wreak on our financial system alone . . .

The more I considered it, the stronger I felt that this was connected somehow. No wonder Dane wanted to know what was going on here. Not to stop it, of course. He had no concern for the economy. I'd lived with him for over a year. I knew better than anyone that his only interest was how something could be used. Or someone.

Today I was that someone. Tomorrow I would wipe my record clean and break free of my uncle's hold forever. I would find his precious intel, fulfill the mission, and pull my mom out from under Dane's thumb once and for all. What Dane did with his intel wasn't my problem.

I tried not to think about Legacy as I left the room.

FOURTEEN
LEGACY

MILLIAN PLOPPED down beside me for breakfast again, going off about the texture of Neuromen's potatoes and how they were cutting corners in reheating yesterday's fake meat. I listened for a couple of minutes before pulling up the day's schedule.

Then I stiffened. *"Blood work?"*

Millian's lips thinned, and I realized I'd interrupted her midsentence. "Just a blood draw scheduled for this morning, and then we're free the rest of the day. You didn't hear yesterday's lecture?" She paused and muttered to herself. "No, I guess you didn't."

"Sorry, I'm trying to listen. I'm just a little distracted today."

"Today. Right."

I shot her a guilty grin. "Start over. I'll try my best to listen this time."

She rolled her eyes. "I guess it isn't entirely your fault. I ramble when I'm nervous. We're getting our positions tomorrow, and I'm in fourth place. The first day's exam results had me in first. Those are the only ones that should matter. Not some dumb fitness test."

I'd forgotten about those. Pulling up the chart, I noticed Kole was in position two. Even more surprisingly, I was number six. Strange. Either that "dumb fitness test" counted for an oddly disproportionate total of our placement scores or Virgil had placed me higher than promised. "They'd be stupid to make you an assistant. I bet you're one of the best candidates they've ever had."

Millian's cheeks went pink at the praise. "Seriously. How much can they really tell about us after four days of testing, anyway?"

Not nearly enough. It bothered me Kole was doing so well yet didn't seem to care. Was it an act, or was he truly so smart and athletic and *everything*?

I gave myself a silent chiding. The Firebrand occupied my thoughts far too often these days. "I don't care what the standings say. I'm not taking their blood test." There was no logical reason they needed a new sample. Everyone had blood and DNA records on their public file taken at birth.

"It doesn't hurt that bad. I bet they'll just take some from your finger. Or are you one of those people who fears blood? My aunt faints when she sees it. One time, when we were at a family dinner, my cousin got hurt and . . ."

I let myself fade away once more. She didn't understand. It wasn't blood or needles that had my stomach flopping like a dying fish. My aversion ran much, much deeper. Something related to a memory that had almost become a dream.

Mom and Gram talking. A much younger me, crouched behind a sofa. A string of unfamiliar words that felt like a sword to the heart when their meaning came together. A feeling of betrayal by those who claimed to love me most.

Nope, that blood draw was not happening. Ever.

I tuned back in, nodding attentively until Millian finished her story. "Yeah, it's pretty much like that. I think I'll skip out on this one."

"Skip the draw?" She looked as if I'd suggested setting the lab on fire.

"They can find whatever they want in my file." I felt strangely light-headed now. "I need some air."

"Sure. I'll . . . tell them, I guess."

"Thanks." I stood and dumped my tray before heading out, my legs shaky.

It was quiet when I arrived at the garden.

I stood there among the trees, wondering why I'd come in the first place. It held no more clues for me. I knew no more about who'd written that graffiti message than the day I'd arrived, and Mom's lab refused to reveal its secrets. I was at a dead end with two days remaining before Virgil's broadcast and an uncertain future before me. The facts were scattered puzzle pieces and Virgil was at the center. I just had to figure out how the pieces fit together.

A breeze sent the leaves rustling. It calmed my frayed nerves long enough that I could admit why I'd really come. I was hiding. From the blood test, from the world. No better place to hide than in a forest, fake as this one was.

I lifted my face toward the open sky and sighed, letting myself enjoy its natural warmth for the first time in days.

"I'd ask what you're doing," Kole said from the shadows, "but I'm not sure I want to know."

I jumped and cursed silently. "If you're trying to prove yourself innocent of my stalking accusations, you're failing."

"I was here first. If anything, you're following me around."

"Oh? I suppose hiding in the trees to avoid having your blood drawn is a new habit, then."

"Brand new." He stepped out, letting the shadows fall behind him. "I intend to do the blood draw later. There's something I have to do first."

"Which is?"

"No questions, remember?" He took another step forward. Now he stood right in front of me, close enough I could see a vein flexing in his jaw. His usual cockiness had been replaced with something quieter, something I couldn't quite place. Something that made my stomach flip in a weird way.

"*If* you didn't stalk me. Now we're right back where we started."

"Where's that, exactly?"

If my heart was racing before, it was downright sprinting now. "That sounds an awful lot like a question."

"It's the only exception to the rule. You said we started in one place, which implies we must be headed to a different one. I'd like to know where that is." His teasing tone was gone now. There was a seriousness to his question that held me captive. There would be no joking my way out of this.

He felt it too. Whatever *it* was.

I'd only felt that pull once before.

Derik.

The name unlocked something inside me, allowing me to tear my eyes free of his gaze and take a step back. "I don't think—"

"Kole Baby," a voice cooed from the hallway door. Zenye bounded over and threw herself between us, her back to me. "Sorry I'm late. It's so hard to get away from those whiny candidates sometimes."

"Hello to you too," I muttered, then choked as she pulled Kole's bewildered face to hers. *Kissing* him. Her hands ran up his chest as she deepened the kiss, her fingers tangling themselves in his hair.

I whirled and stalked out to hide the flush rising from my neck. If he was waiting for his girlfriend, why not say so like a normal person? Why walk toward me like a panther and speak all low and quiet, like there was some kind of secret between us?

Why look at me like *that*?

I stormed into the hallway with clenched fists, putting as much space between the happy couple and myself as possible. This twisted obsession with Kole had to stop. Now.

Pulling up an old mental trick, I gathered any attraction I had for the guy and imagined shoving it into a giant bag. I tied it closed, then tossed it out an imaginary window. Somehow the window became Mom's lab, and the bag landed with a splash in the water beneath, sinking slowly to its death at the bottom of the bay.

It was precisely what Kole Mason deserved. Firebrands toyed with their prey. They got what they wanted through lies and deceit. I, on the other hand, was a Hawking. He would get no satisfaction from me.

With Kole's face flung from my thoughts, it was Derik's lopsided grin that entered. Mom had already begun to grow faceless in my memories, a phenomenon the therapist said was normal. But somehow, every centimeter of Derik's face was burned into my brain forever. Every expression, every fleck of blue in his impossibly light eyes. The inflection in his voice when he talked, the feel of his fingers on my cheek. The softness of his lips on mine.

Somehow it was the memories I most wanted to forget

that clung the tightest, seizing me like a rope around my chest squeezing the breath from my very soul. And it was the memories I longed for most that slipped like air through my fingers.

True to Virgil's word, the door clicked open the moment I reached Mom's lab. I'd almost hoped it was a lie, yet here the room stood. Empty. Quiet. My footsteps echoed as I entered. Everything was just as I'd left it—the shiny metal table in the center, the backless stool. Any evidence of Mom's presence was long gone.

I placed myself on that stool and stared down at my reflection. It should have shown Mom's face with her silly goggles instead. It should have been covered with wires and tiny circuit boards and jars of gray brain matter. She should still be here.

"I still leave the light on sometimes," I told the empty air. "And when I wake up in the morning, it's still on."

The silence absorbed my words until they faded out of existence. There would be no answer, not even here.

It was too quiet. A person could drown in their thoughts in such a room. *A useless lab.* It existed for looks, not function. While the other labs served their scientists in forging new projects that would change human neurotech forever, this one remained empty and alone. Watched, spoken about perhaps, yet avoided entirely. Maybe that was what drew me to it.

This is sick, Legacy, I chided myself. If I meant to stay at Neuromen, it was time to stop sulking. Mom was gone, Dad had essentially removed himself from my life, and Alex couldn't care less about anyone but himself. That meant I had to find my own family. Right here.

Millian would be a good start.

I let myself out the door, ensuring it locked behind me,

before making my way quietly down the hallway. I would hide in the dorms until the silly blood draw was over with. When Millian returned, I would tell her my purpose here. With any luck, she would join the cause.

It wasn't until I'd turned the first corner that I heard the footsteps.

I pushed Zenye off. "What was that?"

"A present. Hope you enjoyed it."

I should have. I'd kissed plenty of girls, the most recent being a neighbor girl just a few weeks ago. But guilt and irritation twisted in my gut now. Legacy's expression burned like a brand into my memory. Hurt. Betrayal.

"I prefer to know a girl at least twenty-four hours first," I muttered.

"That was a very tame kiss. Lucky for you, it didn't take any more to get the message across." She ran her finger up my chest. "I don't know if you could have handled more."

I shoved her hand away. "That was about Legacy."

"Good. Maybe you're smart after all."

I waited a full five seconds before responding, letting the anger recede. "You're wrong about her. She can't stand me or any other Firebrand walking this planet. No threat from her whatsoever."

"Hawkings are always threats, and you're missing the point. I didn't protect you from her. I protected you from yourself."

I gritted my teeth. "I do not like Legacy Hawking."

"Right. I've seen how you look at her. And by the way, you look at her a *lot*."

That couldn't be true. "I'm weighing my enemy."

"There may be some weighing going on, but not the kind you think. Look, I'm not convinced you understand how dangerous she can be to our plans. If this continues, I may have to tell your uncle."

Our plans? What was with this girl?

My frustration finally erupted. "In case you forgot, I'm paying you for this. Me. So take me to this mysterious relay station so we can get this done, or the deal is off."

She lifted her hands in surrender, but the smirk on her face only deepened. "Let's go, then, *boss*."

I EXPECTED to be led outside to a transport and travel across town. Instead, Zenye took me straight to the locked wing, the door clicking open when we arrived. A thrill ran through me as we walked through.

Now I understood. Director Virgil wasn't relying on a nearby relay station to transmit and receive implant data. He had his own station right here—and I was about to see it for myself.

"Getting you past the front desk will be the hardest part," Zenye said, prancing down a white hall that looked identical to the others. "Once we arrive, I'll set back the security camera exactly ten minutes. You'll have that long to make your changes and not a second more, or an alarm sounds and Director Virgil sees you in all your glory."

"Wait. I thought you were doing the actual changing."

"The technician will show you how to create your

record. It won't be hard for an emerging neurotechnician like you. Much faster than you leaning over my shoulder, and that way we won't miss anything."

"Create?"

"You don't actually *change* your record. That would trigger an alarm. You simply create a second record and merge it with yours. The system creates accidental duplicates all the time, so it allows for that without detection."

A new fear gripped me. I halted, pulling her to a stop. "Hold on. I'm paying you to take the risk for me. If I get caught, I'll be arrested."

Her eyes were laughing now. "Don't worry, nobody will notice you. I bring male guests through there all the time."

I didn't want to know what kind of "guests" those were. Yesterday's determination was little more than a trickle now. I hadn't anticipated the risks nor the feeling of finality now taking hold. Creating a new identity for myself meant part of me would cease to exist. The part that knew Mom and had a family, a childhood.

I'm doing this for *Mom,* I reminded myself.

Except it wasn't quite true. Deep down, I knew there was a selfish element to my actions today. A fresh start meant it would be even easier to hide my secret. Few would make the connection between me and my father, and if they chose to expose me, there would be no evidence.

If there were ever a reason to sever myself from my past, that was it.

Zenye watched me expectantly.

I nodded. "Lead the way."

SIXTEEN
KOLE

THEY COULDN'T PUT the relay station near the front desk. That would be too easy. Instead, they'd placed it at the far corner of the top floor. That could be to minimize interference and allow easy access to the station's equipment on the roof, or it could be simply to dissuade unwelcome visitors. Either way, it took a full ten minutes of brisk walking to get there. I'd been wrong about the snowflake thing. This wing was far larger than the others.

The clerk at a huge glass desk glared at Zenye. "What do you think you're doing?"

Zenye placed her head against my arm. "Bringing a guy to see my office. This one's a top three."

Her office?

I stared at her in confusion, but the clerk just rolled his eyes and waved us on.

She practically yanked me down the main hallway before stopping at an extra-wide metal door. Four sharp knocks later, she finally released me and waited, tapping her foot.

An old man opened the door and scowled at us. "What?"

Zenye was all sugar again. "Aw, Ben. Do you have to be so stereotypical all the time?"

He ignored her comment. "Another one?"

"Yep. You good for it?"

"I s'pose. Not too busy today."

She placed a hand on my back and shoved me inside. "Good. I'll be back to pick him up in nine minutes."

I glared at her back as she sauntered off. Twenty-five thousand credits, and I was doing all the work.

Ben closed the door behind me. "Thinks she owns the place, that girl. Let's see what you have to hide." He strode to a messy desk below a clear window that overlooked the bay. Then he began swiping at the inlaid glass.

"The guard didn't question her at all," I said, puzzled by his comment. "How is that possible?"

"Virgil lets her go where she wants. So you're Dane's nephew. Not an affiliation I'd brag about either." Ben shoved his chair back to make room for my approach. I stared at the screen, fascinated to see how much information they had on me. All my previous messages, images, schoolwork, location points. My family records went back a full four generations since the original NORA.

The Filter icon wasn't lit. Good. Assuming I didn't blow my cover in the next eight minutes, whatever intel I discovered here could be sent to "Ned" without worry of interception.

Ben hit a few buttons, and a blank profile page came up next to the first. The two files would be combined, but it was still disconcerting to see it so empty. Then he stood, motioning for me to take his seat. "Have at it."

It seemed too easy. "You sure nobody will know?"

"Just you, me, and Zenye. Our loyalty is to credits, not the law. Politicians use this loophole all the time. But be reasonable in how you fill those fields. Make yourself sound too perfect or too strange, and someone will get suspicious."

"Fair enough." My voice was calm, but a storm brewed inside me. Politicians changed their records? If Uncle Dane knew such a thing was possible, he'd immediately look for evidence that Hawking was doing exactly that. This could destroy the man's career.

And Legacy's livelihood in the process.

It shouldn't have bothered me. It never had before. Yet I felt guilty considering such a thing, and guiltier that I felt bad about it. If Hawking was acting illegally, didn't the country deserve to know? What right did I have to deprive the nation of a prosperous future because of one girl who could barely stand to look at me?

The first thing I did was create a new father. I made him exactly what he should have been—attentive, kind, a good provider. There was nothing in this new record about arrests, prison terms, beatings, or implant-hacking charges. Most importantly, there was no record of his suspicious death or any suspects. That was exactly the way I wanted it.

Replacing Mom's name was harder. I created a variation on her name and pulled a random profile capture out of a miscellaneous file I'd created last night.

"Do you happen to know anything about the new update?" I asked casually as I worked. Ben continued to look over my shoulder, watching every stroke of my fingers on the glass.

"If I did, I wouldn't tell you. Virgil would have my head. He's terrified the word will get out, you know."

Odd. A relay technician with no regard for the law but

scared of Virgil. "Must be one heck of an update, then. New features?"

"I'm sure that'll be the least of it. Assuming Hawking doesn't have his way and shut us down first. If it weren't for that cabinet of his, we'd all be out of a job. His own daughter, even."

Something told me Legacy wouldn't be as broken-hearted about that as people assumed. Not that I cared. "You could transfer to a different relay station. Your skills will always be in demand."

"Not after this update. The government will flood the centers with their own workers and toss us out on our backsides." He turned in a huff and crossed the room.

Government workers? That didn't make much sense. Maybe Uncle Dane could make something of it. I jotted a quick note in my implant files and looked over my shoulder. Ben faced the window, his arm lifted and head tilted back as if he were drinking something. My babysitter was finally distracted.

I finished my work, launched the combine feature, and read through the record. Nothing of any concern here. Perfect.

Then I pulled up my mother's file.

Her prognosis was still "uncertain." At least she wasn't doing any worse. Thinking quickly, I pulled up a new record and cleared her ties to Dad and me. Then I removed her employee information and listed her as "unassigned." I was stuck here, but now she would be eligible to be hired elsewhere. Now I just had to get her transferred closer to me so I could protect her.

I paused, then called up Legacy's file, her face filling the screen. She wasn't smiling, but there was an amused light to her eyes that made her look mischievous. The braid wrapped around her loose hair softened the expression.

Ben would return any second, and I'd been staring too long. I scanned through her records. Parents' names; twin brother, Alex; school records; hobbies. Her information was far more detailed than mine. The record keepers kept a close eye on her.

I scanned the data, feeling guilty all the while. A hospital visit when she was eight. Bi-monthly psychological treatments beginning at age thirteen. An internship offer at her father's office two years ago, which she'd declined. No answers to the question of why she was here.

Buried on a third page was her implant information. It contained her public files. Private files existed by name, but they were blocked off just like everyone else's. At least she had that.

In the bottom corner lay a red icon I hadn't seen before, shaped like a star. Curious, I tapped it.

A security feed pulled up. It showed Legacy walking down a white hallway alone. When she turned a corner, the view immediately switched to show her from a different angle. An auto-tracking system. A tiny digital clock in the corner showed the current time. Strange. My record hadn't offered that option. Virgil had a special interest in keeping Legacy safe, then. Or was it something more?

I was about to exit the page when I stopped short. A figure watched her from around the corner. The moment she turned, the man followed.

I swore.

A fist slammed on the monitor, shutting it down. Then Ben slowly turned his head to face me. "That isn't your record, son."

"Sorry. I finished early, so I checked on a friend."

Inside, I felt an edge of panic. I knew exactly who that figure was. Worse, I knew what he intended to do.

"Get out." Ben grabbed the back of the chair and practically pulled it out from under me.

I didn't argue. The hallway was still empty when I stumbled outside. I didn't wait for Zenye. I just plunged down the hall at a half run, sending a wave to the clerk at the desk. I didn't slow to see whether he noticed.

Then I sprinted for the lab wing.

SEVENTEEN
LEGACY

I paused in the hallway and listened, every muscle taut. The footsteps had stopped, yet I knew better than to ignore my instincts. And every instinct I possessed screamed that something was very wrong.

A large, sweaty hand covered my mouth and yanked me backward.

I growled and wrenched my head around, trying to free myself, but my attacker used the momentum to slam me against the wall, knocking the wind from my lungs.

A desperate gasp escaped my throat as hands closed over my shoulders and shoved me hard again. Creepy Boy from the party. He'd followed me somehow.

Then his mouth covered mine—hard.

I was too much in shock to respond. This couldn't possibly be happening. Not now, when I was utterly and completely alone.

I lifted my knee to strike his groin, but he stepped in closer, crushing me under his weight. So *heavy*.

Hundreds of personal training hours, and here I was,

pinned between a wall and a man who refused to ask, much less take no for an answer.

Wrenching my head to one side, I managed to break contact and pull one shoulder free. It was enough to shove him back a few centimeters.

I gasped, sucking in precious air as he grinned. "They may paint you as a good little girl, but we both know better."

I wanted to spit in his face, but that would involve gathering saliva, which seemed a repulsive act at the moment, the taste of him still overwhelming my mouth. Instead, I lifted my hands between us and slipped into fighting stance. "Leave. Me. Alone."

He took another step forward. "You resent Daddy. I can tell. Your brother falls in line, but you don't, do you? All the rules and guards and the press following you around. I can help you escape all of it." He reached for my head.

I batted his hand away and threw a wild punch. He ducked it easily and grinned wider. Then he was on me again, his foul breath on my face, mouth searching for mine.

I growled and threw all my strength into freeing myself, but he grabbed my throat and slammed my head against the wall. Darkness and glittery stars exploded into my vision, obscuring the implant time. My legs would have buckled altogether had he not held me up with his weight.

He whispered against my lips. "That's better."

"I'll make sure you don't wake up tomorrow," I hissed, still fighting the stars flying across my vision. I freed an elbow and sent it sailing toward his head, but he released my face and caught it before it connected. Then he wrenched my arm, making me gasp.

I was done. I lifted my foot and slammed it down onto his shoe. He flinched as I sailed my knee into his manly parts.

He grunted and bent over, stiff as a statue. Finally.

As I broke free and sprinted down the hallway, I heard a fist slam into the wall behind me, followed by another grunt and the sound of hopping.

I took the turn at a sprint, hitting the opposite wall with my shoulder. My breath came out in a series of gasps and bursts, and I spat out the taste of that horrible man again and again. My room was only a few turns away, wasn't it? But he would expect me to go there and find me . . . *fates.* My desperate attempt to put space behind me had muddled my head. *Think.*

My legs struggled to hold me, and I found myself tripping. I landed in a heap at the next turn and struggled to my shaky feet once again. Straightening my shirt, I fought a surge of nausea. Angry tears collected beneath my eyelids. I wanted to take a boiling-hot shower and down a giant bottle of mouthwash.

It wasn't safe here. I had to keep going.

Several more turns. Where was the women's corridor again?

"Legacy!"

I jumped before realizing it was Kole, not Creepy Guy. Allowing myself to slow down, I kept my face turned away. "What?"

He ducked to meet my gaze. Beads of sweat appeared on his forehead, his eyes wide with concern. He was breathing nearly as hard as I was. "Legacy. Please tell me you're okay."

No. I wasn't okay, nor would I be anytime soon. My panic-riddled brain tried to form the words, but nothing escaped my lips. Instead, I threw myself into his arms.

He stiffened for only a fraction of a second before tightening the embrace, one hand stroking my hair. I trembled against his body, taking in the light perspiration and soap scent of his shirt. I hadn't been held like this in so long.

Derik came to mind, then faded away into nothingness.

Finally, my brain caught up with me, and it registered that Kole wasn't asking the questions I expected. I pulled away and gathered my composure around me like a blanket. "You knew."

His jaw tightened, his expression stony in a way I'd never seen. Now *that* was the face of a Firebrand. Yet it warmed me in a way I couldn't explain. His hands curled into slow, tight fists. "I saw Lars following you. He has this obsession—I've already tried talking to him, but it obviously wasn't enough. Next time I see him, I'll rip his bloody head from his body."

I wanted nothing more, but I had to remember who Kole was. I put that internal wall up once again. "Actually, I plan to do that myself. But I'll save you an arm if you like."

"Brutal. I like that." He lifted a hand to my shoulder, hesitated, and dropped it again. "Are you really okay? Maybe we should take you to the nurse."

"No. I mean, yes, I'm okay. I fought him off before he . . ." The next words were unthinkable. Those types of things happened to women in the Shadows, not heiresses at science labs.

It shouldn't happen to anyone, I stubbornly told myself. No woman deserved to be treated like that, whether from the Shadows or anywhere else.

I half expected another lecture from Kole about wandering off alone, but he placed himself at my side. "Then I'm walking you to your room. I'm telling Director Virgil about this, and I won't sleep until Lars is behind bars."

I wanted to laugh. A Firebrand sworn to protect me.

Dad would have me committed if he could hear my thoughts right now. "Thanks, but I'll file the report myself." I'd include enough details to have Creepy Guy—Lars—removed, but not enough to imply that I couldn't defend myself. I wasn't done here yet, and I certainly didn't need any guards following me around.

We fell in step as we moved toward a smaller hallway to the left, one I now recognized. In my panic, I'd chosen the wrong route. My shaking had stopped, but a new chill ran through my body at the memory of Kole's face when he called my name. It wasn't the expression of a guy who'd just enjoyed a thorough make-out session with his girlfriend. It was the desperation of someone who really and truly cared.

"Have fun with Zenye?" I asked casually.

He groaned. "She came on to me, I swear. Zenye isn't my type at all."

"You didn't seem too shaken up about it."

"Then you didn't stick around for the finale. If she were a guy, she'd have a purple eye right now."

I shouldn't have believed him, but there was authenticity in everything about him—his voice, the way he moved, his sharp gaze when it fell upon me. It made my breath catch a little. "Because you're the type who kisses girls, not the other way around."

He snickered. "You twist everything I say against me. Must be a hidden talent."

"Not so hidden. I have preconceived notions about all Firebrands, so it isn't just you." I cocked my head. "You mean to tell me what really happened?"

His shoulders went stiff. "What do you mean?"

"If you'd really seen Lars following me, you would have followed a minute or two behind. Instead, you came puffing up like you've run across the entire lab."

He tore his gaze away. "I can't explain that."

"Do you know about the graffiti warning in the garden on the first day? Or the smear of blood?"

Kole looked confused. "Blood?"

He didn't know. Disappointment nearly shut my mouth for good, but I suddenly felt a need for him to understand. "Clues in my investigation. I visited my mom's lab before Lars found me, looking for evidence as to what really happened the day she died."

Kole paused and turned to face me, looking thoughtful. His uniform made his eyes more of a dark blue than the gray I'd noticed earlier. Almost the opposite of Derik's.

"That's why you're here," he whispered.

I nodded.

He looked down the hall. First one way, then the other. After a moment's hesitation, he spoke again. "Legacy, I shouldn't be telling you this, but I think Director Virgil knows what you're doing. Or at least he suspects. He's having you watched."

I glanced at the camera at the next corner. "He's watching everyone."

"No, I mean he's tracking your implant. He's watching your activities, your location, who you speak with. Your very presence here is a threat to him."

I stared at him, this boy I barely knew who pretended to care so convincingly that I felt safe with him. "And you know all this because of the thing you can't say?"

He flinched and turned away. "Sorry."

I stepped forward, closing the distance between the Firebrand and myself. He didn't move. He just waited, his eyes searching my face for any hint of my intentions.

"Why are you telling me this?" I asked softly.

He met my gaze with a steady one of his own. "Because

I wish our families weren't enemies. Because I know who you are, and it's not who they see. Because you're more than just a Hawking."

There were mere centimeters between us now, warm and crackling, like a lit match. It was like we'd taken to the track once more—stride for stride, neither engaging nor admitting defeat.

The moment stretched into an eternity and back again. He dared to exhale. I felt the warmth of it on my face.

I didn't know what he was, but I wanted to. That scared me more than anything.

Folding my arms across my chest, I took two steps back. "I need to get going."

Disappointment flooded his expression, but he hid it immediately. "Of course. After what you just went through . . . I'm an idiot for keeping you here."

"Stay. I'll be fine." I started to walk away, then turned back. "When people look at me, they see a role, not a person. I can't be used again. I won't."

He shrugged. "I get it. Better than you think."

I didn't let myself ponder what that meant. I just left him standing there, my head dizzy from the earlier adrenaline rush followed by . . . whatever had just happened.

Kole followed me back at a respectful distance. When I was safely in my room, I placed my back against the door and leaned my head against it, listening. No sound.

His footsteps finally retreated an hour later.

EIGHTEEN

LEGACY

A HAND SHOOK MY SHOULDER. "Hey, roomie." Another shake. "Legacy."

I smacked the hand off and rolled away before prying my eyes open. The bedroom was bright with new light, my roommate was fully dressed, and the scent of shampoo mingled with steam filled the air.

Morning.

Millian walked to the dresser. "You fell asleep sitting up, facing the door. Judging by the barricade of pillows and blankets around you, something's up. You don't usually sleep through the alarm, either. Here. Food fixes everything." She handed me a heaping tray of breakfast foods. Like, every single one. Three kinds of biscuits, pancakes in two styles, a pile of fruit, and a big chunk of meat next to a boiled egg. "Wasn't sure what you like. The 'meat' is actually pretty decent today. Must have fired the old cook or something."

As she pulled back her arm, I caught sight of those angry gashes in her wrist again. She followed my gaze and pulled her sleeve down, her cheeks reddening.

"Thank you," I said softly. There was enough food here for three people, but my stomach grumbled its approval. Her thoughtfulness reminded me of my mom all over again.

"See, now you're getting all misty and thanking me for things. I'm not leaving until you tell me what's wrong." She plopped herself down on her bed and folded her legs.

I distantly remembered my resolution to tell Millian everything last night, but it felt like a lifetime ago. That Legacy felt like a different girl altogether.

They may paint you as a good little girl, but we both know better.

Derik's work. Lars wasn't the only guy who'd seen that awful interview about our relationship. He was just the first to feel entitled enough to act on Derik's horrible accusations.

"Wow. This must be really bad. You're never at a loss for words." Millian leaned forward. "Does this have anything to do with that guy who got arrested last night?"

"Arrested?"

"Yep. A group of enforcers raided the cafeteria at dinner. Remember Kole from school? They questioned him, but it was his roommate they arrested. The creepy guy from the party. Kole looked really angry. He wasn't at breakfast this morning."

I bit into a piece of the fake breakfast meat. Millian was right—it wasn't bad. "Kole wasn't upset that his roommate got arrested. He was upset because of what Lars did. Or tried to do." Kole must have filed his report anyway while I huddled under my blankets last night. I should have been irritated that he hadn't listened, but I didn't mind so much today.

Millian's face drained of color. "Fates. Lars didn't . . ."

"He tried. I fought him off. I ran into Kole afterward,

and he escorted me back." My stomach churned at the memory. As good as the meat smelled, I moved on to the fruit.

"*Fates!*" She launched herself off the bed and threw her arms around me. When she pulled away, her face was purple. "Good thing they hauled him off before I could strangle him 'cause I really want to right now. To think I was running in circles on the track last night, trying to keep my spot in the standings and completely oblivious."

"This wasn't your fault. Lars gets all the blame."

She nodded her head vigorously. "Definitely. Here's the deal, then. Neither of us wanders the halls alone. If one of us leaves, so does the other."

"I don't need protection. I came here to escape all of that."

A glint appeared in her eye. "Oh? Silly me. I thought it was to uncover the mystery of your mom's death."

I froze with a grape halfway raised to my mouth. It dropped to the plate before I could catch it. "What?"

She beamed, looking victorious. "I knew it. You don't like science, and I don't think you're the type to come just to get away from your dad. You keep wandering around alone like you're looking for something. It doesn't take a top neuroscientist to put all the pieces together, you know." A chuckle. "But then, since that's what I am . . ."

For the first time since last night's events, I smiled. It felt really good. "Should've known better than to try and fool you."

"Seriously. Scientists see everything." She gave me a stern look. "But really, whatever you feel like sharing stays between us. Maybe I can help with my genius brain and all."

My smile faded. "I should have involved you from the

start. I just kept thinking about Derik, my ex, and it scared me off. He actually told me something similar once."

"No," she said in mock horror. "He has a genius brain too?"

I chuckled.

She sobered, tucking her legs beneath her. "Sorry. I have issues. Tell me about him."

I did. Derik was the perfect friend from a perfect family, some high-society friends of my dad's. He'd had a high-paying job lined up for him after graduation. He'd been everything I wanted and everything the gossip broadcasts deemed acceptable for an heiress. We spent every spare moment of several weeks together. It felt so good to finally be myself with someone, to talk about things I couldn't discuss with Mom or the rest of my family. It was a relief to remove the heavy armor I'd carried around my entire life and set it aside for a while, trusting another person completely.

Then I'd woken one morning to find a capture of my face on an exclusive broadcasting station. My boyfriend sat next to an announcer, dumping my dreams and fears upon a hungry public for a few thousand credits and an hour of fame.

When he ran out of the true stuff, the lies began.

As I talked, one thing became clear. I'd been right to reject Kole. Derik had managed to slip through a tiny crack in my heart before slashing it to bloody ribbons. How much worse could a secretive Firebrand do? He'd already admitted that he couldn't answer my questions. His group clearly came first. I wasn't even a distant second. I'd been a fool to let the slightest hint of a crack appear in my armor yesterday.

And, yet, instead of taking advantage of my vulnerability, he'd stood watch by my door and had Lars arrested. Surely that meant something.

When I finished, Millian looked stunned. "Wow."

"Yeah."

She sat back. "No, I'm serious. What kind of boyfriend gets you to trust him, then turns around and sells lies about you to the press?"

"A really bad one." Kole was a Firebrand, and I knew deep down that even he wouldn't do that.

You're more than a Hawking.

"So," I began, more than ready to change the subject. "I just vomited my soul on you. If you ever want to talk about those scars on your arm, I'm here."

Millian quickly pulled her sleeve down, blushing once again. "Um, maybe another time. Not that I don't trust you. I know I need to quit, and I will. It's just that this . . . habit . . . helped me get through some tough times at home. It might take a while."

"If it helps, I'm here to listen anytime. Seriously."

"Thanks." She gave me an uncharacteristically shy smile. "What are you going to do now? I mean, you really should take the day off. Light schedule again. Some lecture about lab safety and then the standings announcement tonight. Go into town and visit your family or maybe go back to bed. I'll tell everyone you're sick."

Climbing back into bed sounded really nice. But sometime during the past twenty minutes, the fire in my chest had ignited again.

I set the tray aside and stood, heading for the full-sized mirror at the end of the room. It showed a disheveled version of me in all my yesterday's-clothes-and-bedhead glory. There was fear in that Legacy's eyes as she peered back at me. Fear, mistrust, and helplessness. A pampered girl who'd tasted real life and recoiled from it rather than attacking it head-on. Someone who hid from her problems, burying herself in misery.

Dad had chosen that route. I knew exactly where that led.

"I need a run to clear my head," I told her and retrieved a clean shirt from the drawer.

"You're going out?" Millian asked incredulously. "Now?"

"Now. Come or stay, whatever you want. Running helps me focus." Kole believed Virgil knew my purpose here. If so, Virgil had to know I suspected him. I intended to pick apart his lies one at a time until I saw where he fit in all this.

Millian made a face. "I ran yesterday and the day before. I'm good for the next year. But we agreed to stick together out there, so I'll come anyway. I have a few hacks I use to dig into the IM-NET storage servers. Maybe they have some hidden files about your mom's accident—er, whatever it was."

"Murder. I'm certain of it." I'd never voiced it aloud before. The fire inside me flared at the words until heat pumped through my veins. "Okay, let's go."

A COUPLE CHATTED while lifting weights in the alcove, barely noticing Millian approaching a distant bench. Squat windows lit sections of the track like beacons that beckoned me onward.

I quickly stretched, then set my pace at a slow jog. It felt so good to move like this. I'd spent most of yesterday in a tight, curled-up position on my bed, the nightmarish events of the morning on replay in my head. Home or here, there would be people ready to use me. Virgil and Lars had already made that clear.

Kole obviously had connections to the lab's security. That meant the Firebrands were working with Virgil. How could a lab director possibly help an activist group take over the government? Did it have anything to do with this update announcement tomorrow? Was he slipping something illegal into the software? Something told me that Kole wouldn't be a part of that if he knew. Though with Firebrands, it was impossible to tell for sure.

I passed the spot where Kole had cheated to win our little running contest and let myself smile.

"Legacy!"

I pulled up short, my momentum nearly taking me into the wall nearest the weights alcove. Millian stood there, lowering her cupped hands from her mouth.

"I've been calling you for two minutes. Fates. That must have been an intense broadcast."

I never watched shows while I ran, but I also couldn't explain where my thoughts had been, so I let it pass. "What?"

"I found an interview with your mom in the history archives. Have you seen it?"

"I'm not sure." I'd seen plenty of her public interviews, but they were all the same—Director Virgil announcing some award she'd won and attributing it to the "high quality" of his employees. They didn't exactly have options when it came to neurotechnology. Virgil's lab had beaten out every one of his competitors.

"IM-NET 4416 dated CC52. She comes in at the 5:51 mark."

I stumbled to a bench and sat down before pulling up

the broadcast, my legs shaking more than they should as I conducted a quick search.

It took a few minutes of scrolling before I found it. Virgil wasn't present this time. I wondered whether he even knew about it.

Mom took up the entire length of the screen. The suddenness of her face sent a jolt down my system. It was perhaps four years ago, before she'd grown her dark hair down her back. It hung in soft waves around her face, contrasting her prominent dimpled chin. Her blue Neuromen uniform boasted a gold patch with "Research Head" in bold lettering.

" . . . wouldn't say it's all that confusing," she said and then chuckled. "People have an inherent fascination with machines. In the beginning, we asked if machines could do the same things we could. Then we asked if machines could do the things we *couldn't* do. Now that we've unharnessed the incredible potential of technology, the question is whether we can merge both elements into something greater than the sum of their parts. I believe the answer is yes."

I felt a different pain now. The combining of human and machine—the singularity, as Mom called it—was a favorite dinnertime discussion of hers. We smiled and asked questions, but ultimately, I'd always assumed it to be a scientist's fantasy.

This was her project. I knew it down to the aching muscles in my legs protesting my sudden immobility. While Virgil focused on implants that connected us, Mom had spent over a decade working on implants that enhanced us. She'd hinted at it around the dinner table a hundred times. How had I missed it?

The off-screen interviewer spoke up. "You say it's

possible to combine the two. How exactly would that work?"

"Brain implant tech, or neurotechnology, is the foundation. We've harnessed the inner workings of the human brain. This part is far more technical than most realize. It involves a complex understanding of the brain's vision and hearing centers as well as modified electrical components. If you take a step back and really look at how the body is built, it's almost mathematic in its origin." Mom flushed. "Pardon me. This is the point where my family would ask me to speak English. Let me try again."

The interviewer laughed. "I'm with you, but please continue however you'd like."

"Let's just say technology and the human body were never opposites. They can enhance one another. We discovered this with our recent exploration into sports, as you'll recall."

I remembered the scandal from a few years back. An athlete had discovered that rewiring his implant made his khel reaction time faster. He'd been disqualified, but the discovery had created a huge rush for the technology on the black market.

"There are other unexpected benefits. Hormone alteration, boosting the immune system, the eradication of cancer, and even solving reproductive issues. We've repaired many of the human body's failings with neurotech."

"All incredible breakthroughs," the interviewer said. "But what you're working on takes it a step further."

"It does."

"Can you elaborate on how?"

Mom straightened and smiled at the camera. "Absolutely. I've discovered the ultimate use for neurotech. It's far more important and even more promising than the medical advancements we've seen over the past two decades."

"Which is?"

Her smile turned into a smirk. "I'm afraid I can't elaborate yet. I hope to announce it very soon."

"Now you're teasing us, Dr. Hawking," the interviewer said, but I detected an element of flirtation in his tone. He was only feigning irritation.

"It's unfortunate I can't outline everything I've found so far, that's true. But the problem is that young scientists are emulating and experimenting with implant technology, and I don't want to give them ideas that could end up harming them or others. In the wrong hands, this breakthrough could be dangerous. In the right hands, it can change the world."

"Do you consider yourself the right hands, Dr. Hawking?"

"I certainly hope so. Otherwise, I don't deserve to have this knowledge."

"We look forward to your next announcement, then. Thanks for joining us today."

I closed the broadcast and stared at nothing for a moment. The wrong hands. Something deep inside told me Mom's hands were the right ones . . . and Director Virgil's were the wrong ones. Yet she was dead and he was about to announce a new implant update, something revolutionary. Was he about to release Mom's experiment into the world and take credit?

Had he killed her for it?

"You look like you're going to beat someone up," Millian said, sitting on the bench beside me. "I'll make a few suggestions on victims if you want, but please don't hurt me."

I wasn't in the mood to joke. The man who'd described

Mom's death to my family, fighting tears, had been the very one to take her from us. Having a head researcher develop a powerful new update as her job required was too much of a threat for him. Hadn't he tried to take credit for the invention of brain implants in the first place? Gram kept insisting they'd been used in Europe long before she'd become the leader of NORA. I'd ignored that too.

"Everything Virgil told me was a lie," I told her, my voice shaking. "I think he stole her experiment and killed her to pass it off as his own. It's what he's announcing tomorrow. It has to be."

Millian frowned. "Tomorrow?"

"At a broadcast announcement. He asked me to deliver the news, actually." Now I understood. It had little to do with public relations. This was about his biggest rival—my father. Dad had to know something about this, and Virgil wanted him silenced. What better way to do that than use his own daughter against him?

Virgil would answer for this one way or another.

Because I would not be used again.

NINETEEN

KOLE

Despite my best efforts at distraction, Legacy Hawking occupied my thoughts all the next day. Her face was on my mind during my morning run. I barely remembered eating lunch despite my hunger. I put my shoes on wrong and almost forgot my way around Neuromen's mazelike hallways. The one thing that could persuade my brain to focus on anything else was Mom's situation.

I wasn't sure which subject was more miserable.

That afternoon, I shot off a quick message to Dane about the update announcement tomorrow and a recap of Ben the technician's employment fears. I said nothing of Legacy and her intense security. All that remained was to find the money for a hospital transfer. Mom wouldn't be truly safe until I helped her disappear. Unfortunately, Zenye had taken a chunk out of my savings. That meant I had to convince Dane to help without him knowing where the money would go.

That evening, I received another message from Ned. It was an order to meet him in the parking lot in ten minutes.

Dane was here.

I found my way to the lobby in a state of dread. There were a dozen possible reasons for his presence—communications weren't as secure as I'd thought, or possibly a desire to express his anger in my inability to discover what the implant update actually did. Or maybe his approval of my work.

I snorted at that. *Not likely.*

A single unmarked transport waited near the front doors. I doubted it was a Firebrand vehicle. The finish was too clean, the interior too nice. I climbed in next to him and was immediately assaulted by the heavy smell of alcohol. His gaze, however, was clear.

"I got your message earlier. It was incomplete, but it confirmed my suspicions. In fact, I've set up a meeting with Virgil in about twenty minutes. This could be very exciting for the cause."

My dread felt like a block of iron now. "That's why you wanted to know what the update did. You intended to join up with him and use his technology."

"Precisely. The timing is a bit early for us considering I have about two hundred new graduates still in training, but we'll accelerate things. My last weapons shipment is due to arrive tomorrow, and most of the Firebrands have given their blood samples already. It should all work out."

I blinked at that. Blood samples?

"Don't look so baffled. I'll handle everything. All you have to do is listen carefully." He leaned forward, forcing me to slump back against the door. "By midnight tomorrow, you'll kidnap the Hawking girl and bring her to me."

The transport felt like it was moving. Or maybe that was my insides shrinking from the terrible words leaving his mouth.

"Kidnap her," I repeated dumbly.

"For a scientist, you sure are dense sometimes. Yes, kidnap her. Or talk her into coming along if you two are as close as that Zori girl says. Just get her to my house by one."

He meant Zenye. She'd reported my relationship with Legacy to Dane. "But why?"

"To force action on her family's part, of course. Why do you think?"

I felt numb. The questions in my head went silent as I tried to grasp this new reality. I was a Firebrand. I'd taken the oath. Rejecting my uncle's order meant death. It meant my body found next to a dumpster or dumped into the ocean.

I couldn't run from this with my mom in the hospital. It was simple—I'd handed Dane control of my life when I accepted that stupid tattoo and took his stupid oath.

"You want to use her," I said through gritted teeth. The words felt like rocks in my throat.

He looked surprised. "Of course. It's like the fates decreed it, sending her here. Now, they say she's a prickly one, so you may have to drug and carry her. Whatever you choose, do it quietly. One of my demands for Virgil—and I think he'll agree—is that his security teams turn a blind eye to your escape. But if anyone else sees you, it's over."

His words barely registered. Two faces took up residence in my mind until I couldn't think about anything else.

Legacy or Mom?

I couldn't have both.

Dane watched me expectantly, his eyes darkening by the second. Fates. If I gave him any reason to doubt my loyalty, it was over anyway.

"Got it," I managed and forced a smile. My insides screamed in protest. This wasn't a choice I could make right now.

"My house by one," he said firmly. "Or I'll visit the hospital shortly afterward." The implication was clear. It didn't take a medical professional to unplug a machine.

He waved me out of the vehicle, an order with which I was happy to comply. I hurried to the doors and shoved my hands deep into my pockets, keeping my head down until I reached the men's dorms once more. My room was empty, devoid of Lars's belongings. They'd finally sent for his things. We'd removed one threat to Legacy only to welcome another.

That threat was me, because one thing was clear.

I would not let my mother die.

THAT NIGHT, I dreamed about Zenye.

She was dragging me down the bright halls of Neuromen, shouting something unintelligible. We emerged onto a huge fight taking place in the lobby. Enforcers wrestled with Firebrands, and bodies lay everywhere. Legacy stood at the center, downing an approaching pair of Firebrands with her fists. She held her own, but there was an underlying exhaustion that led me to believe she'd been fighting for a very long time. One second of distraction or weakness and she was a goner.

Zenye shoved a stunner in my hand and stepped back. "Kill her."

I gaped at the stunner.

Zenye grabbed my arm and aimed the weapon. "Kill her *now*." It was no longer her voice. It was Dane's.

I lowered the weapon. "No."

A hand grabbed me from behind and spun me around.

The man's eyes resembled Dane's, but he had more hair and a straighter jaw. My father.

He slammed me against a wall and got right in my face. "You are my son, and you've taken up my cause. You will not say no when your path is laid out."

It's not your cause. The words wouldn't come out. I was frozen, as I always was with my father around. Nobody spoke like that to Dad or his brother, Dane. They were a fearsome pair.

Except that somewhere in my mind, I remembered that Dad was dead. This had to be a dream. It was that realization that unlocked my tongue so I could speak. "I'm not a murderer."

Dad's eyes were red-rimmed, almost crazy. He swiped the stunner from my hand and placed it against my head. "Then you'll be the one to die."

I waited.

When I didn't respond, Dad's hand relaxed. For a moment, I thought he was bluffing, then I followed his gaze to a newcomer. Mom. She'd just walked in, still wearing her hospital gown with an IV tower following along behind her.

"Kole?" she asked. "What's going on?"

With one smooth movement, Dad swung the stunner to her and pulled the trigger.

I woke up on the floor.

It was hard and cold. Breathing heavily, I checked the time: 05:21. My heart was galloping like an old-fashioned racehorse.

Just a dream. Nothing more.

Only this dream was more disturbing than most. The worst element wasn't the order to kill Legacy or Dad shooting my mom. It was something I'd said.

I'm not a murderer.

I didn't know what bothered me more—the fact that Dad hadn't refuted it or the fact that it was a lie.

TWENTY

KOLE

MY ENTIRE FIFTEEN-YEAR-OLD BODY TENSED, every muscle on alert. I had the hearing of a hunting hound when Dad came home late. I glanced at the clock: 02:03 a.m. The only sound that mattered was the shuffling of objects being moved in the kitchen, a drawer slamming, and then another cupboard being searched. Finally, irregular footfalls squeaked up the stairs. Drunk again.

I dared to take a breath, noticing how my lungs burned. But it wasn't over yet. Soon there would be muffled talking, then one of two things would happen—Dad would fall asleep and the house would plunge into silence once more, or the shouting would begin.

I couldn't make out what my parents were saying through the ceiling overhead. Mom's voice wasn't as tired as it should be. She'd waited up for him.

Something hard slammed onto the floor upstairs. I sat bolt upright, my body tense once more. So much for the hope that he would go to sleep.

Mom grunted and began talking again, softly, as if to an upset child. He hated when she did that. There was another exchange, louder this time. Defensiveness crept into my mother's voice.

I tossed the blankets aside and crept along the floor, avoiding the boards that squeaked. The drawer opened without a sound. I grabbed the stunner hidden beneath my bunched-up shirts and headed toward the stairs.

" . . . is not for you," Dad was saying in slurred speech. "You're worthless. Always taking and demanding more."

"We would've lost the house. Did you want our son to live on the street?"

"You're too scared to ask your boss for a raise. You were always too afraid to do what needed to be done."

"I've tried, and I'll always do what I must to protect this family." She paused. "Even against you."

Another slap. This time Mom hit the wall and slid to the floor. I was halfway up the stairs.

The next strike was a kick. I knew it by the exhalation that burst from my mother's mouth.

My father's voice was a gunshot in the otherwise quiet house. "Don't." Another kick. "You." Kick. "Talk back to me."

"Stop," she squeaked.

He swore. There was a swish of liquid in a packet. It was always worse when he brought the alcohol home. Another late "meeting" with his Firebrand friends.

"Please," she gasped from the floor. "I can't support us alone anymore. I need the man I married to come back to us."

I took my usual place by their open doorway. We'd scraped by on Mom's income my entire life while Dad spent his own. She must have gotten desperate and dipped into his account to pay the bills this month. I didn't realize things had gotten so bad.

He guffawed and tossed the alcohol packet. It hit the wall too. "The man you married was a fool. I've finally discovered what I was meant to do, and it was never this. Dane's opened my eyes to what's possible."

"What, secret murders and kidnappings?" Mom snapped. "That's not how we change things."

I went rigid. Mom knew better than to answer like that when he was drunk. Dad couldn't be reasoned with. He wasn't thinking straight. It made him do things he shouldn't.

Dad went quiet.

I gripped the stolen stunner, feeling its smooth surface slip in the slickness of my sweaty hand. I'd brought the weapon up with me a dozen times on nights just like this one. But the thought of actually using it always rendered my fingers still. There were a dozen excuses—it was dark. I could miss and hit Mom. He would turn and attack me instead. He would remember and take the weapon from me, using it on both of us.

I lowered the weapon.

"Don't—" she cried.

The next blow silenced her completely. I flinched as she hit the floor again and was still.

Dad grumbled under his breath. The clang of a belt buckle broke the silence, and then came the all-too-familiar sound of liquid.

Dad was pissing on my mother.

The rage overcame me then—a rage borne of a hundred nights just like this one. Nights of silent terror that I tried unsuccessfully to forget. Nights that left Mom broken, sometimes in the hospital for days at a time. Nights that would never end so long as I stood watching.

With this stunner, there would be no reason to fear again.

I entered the doorway, weapon lifted. I squinted in the moonlight spilling from the window and found his silhouette near the corner, his back to me.

I leveled the weapon at him.

And pulled the trigger.

THE DAY after my meeting with Dane was the longest of my life. The minutes crawled by. I spent the day checking the windows, waiting for nightfall yet dreading it all at once. By this time tomorrow, it would be over. Legacy would be in the hands of my uncle, and it would be me who put her there. She would never trust me again.

The fact that Mom would be safe—at least for now—somehow didn't make me feel any better.

By the time Neuromen's power mandate hit and the lights dimmed, that massive chunk of iron in my stomach felt heavier than ever.

I waited outside Legacy's room longer than I should have. Finally, I banged my fists on the door, wincing at the noise. It opened in seconds, the relief sweeping across Legacy's face ratcheting up my guilt. She wore a tank top that revealed slender shoulders, sandals, and shorts so short I had to tear my gaze away.

"You know, breaking down a girl's doors is generally considered inconsiderate." She countered the words with a smile. A real one, not the fake camera presence she'd had at our Declarations.

It was a smile I couldn't return. In fact, I struggled to look at her without feeling sick. "Doesn't look like I woke you."

"I was up. Not sleeping well these days." Her smile fled,

replaced by the shadow of anger. I wanted nothing more than to ease the darkness from her features and bring that smile back. Instead, I was here to betray her just like everyone else she knew.

"Can we walk?" I asked.

She shot a look at her roommate and stepped out into the hallway, closing the door behind her. The knife stabbing my gut wrenched itself even deeper. Two days ago, she never would have agreed so quickly. Had so much changed between us? I wondered what more could have changed if it weren't for Dane's new order.

She cocked her head. "Did you wake me up so you could stare at me? Because I already have quite enough of that in my life."

"Sorry. It's just that I couldn't sleep, and I figured you couldn't either, and . . . I just needed someone to talk to." *Idiot.* I sounded like a whiny schoolboy.

"I get that." Her hand brushed mine as we walked. Accidentally? It was hard to tell.

"Are you doing okay? Lars is gone, in case you wondered. The enforcers asked me to tell you they'll need your statement soon."

"I spoke with them earlier, and I'm fine." She paused. "Will they tell my dad?"

"I don't think so. As a legal adult, they would need your permission first."

She nodded. "Good."

I checked the time. A transport would pull up to the front soon, likely the one Dane had hired yesterday. Assuming Virgil kept his bargain, there would be no driver and no witnesses. Nobody would ever know what happened tonight.

Except me. *I* would know.

I fingered the tattoo on my chest, the skin under it still slightly raised and tender. The same tattoo my father had worn. The words of our traditional oath echoed through my mind—words Dad had written.

I will direct the Undiscerning Sun to reach those in the Shadows. I will never stop pushing for change. I will protect my Firebrand family to the loss of my blood or my life. I will enact change in my community until the day I die, no matter the cost.

"You're quiet tonight," Legacy said. Her fingers found my arm, and she pulled me to a stop. Her expression was one of concern. "Are you all right?"

I knew where that oath would take me. I'd already killed my own father. What more would I do before finally deciding who *I* wanted to become? Spying was one thing. Kidnapping was entirely another, especially Legacy Hawking. If caught, it wouldn't be Dane who went to prison. And if I succeeded, I'd spend my life behind invisible bars of my own making. Bars that had once held my father bound.

Dad was *not* what I wanted to become.

I'd joined the Firebrands because I didn't have a choice. But I'd eventually convinced myself I was fighting for equality, helping those who felt stuck in their lives. People like Mom. I still felt strongly that something needed to change, but I knew better than anyone that having my uncle and his Firebrands in charge would be a disaster.

It would mean exchanging one regime for another.

Legacy followed my gaze to the hallway that led to the lobby. "Kole, you're scaring me. What's going on?"

"I can't do it," I said softly.

"Do what?"

"Lie to you. Betray your trust." I swallowed. "Use you like the others."

Her fingers ripped from my arm as she took a step backward, horror spreading across her face. "You'd better explain."

"The leader of the Firebrands, Dane, is my uncle. He ordered me to kidnap you."

She shot a glance down the hallway, but we were alone. I gave her all the space she needed. "But you won't. Because you feel guilty."

"I won't because it's wrong. There are feelings involved, but there shouldn't be."

She took another step back. "So last night, and the day before that. It was all an act?"

I shook my head firmly. "All real. At least for me. I never intended for you to get tangled in this. But my uncle found out I was growing close to you, which also never should have happened. You deserve better."

Her chin rose. "You're right. I do. But any Firebrand plot that hurts my father also hurts me. You need to tell me what they're planning. It has to do with the update, doesn't it?"

I looked around, but we were alone in the darkness. "Dane's a shark. He wouldn't be involved unless he smelled blood. Whatever this update triggers, it will involve violence. If things go well, maybe a peaceful Firebrand takeover of the Block. If they go badly, people will die. I'm betting it will start with your family."

Even in the low light, her eyes were saucers. "Oh."

"Look, you have to leave. Warn your dad and hire more guards for protection. If you can convince your family to stay away from the Block, even better."

She was quiet for a long moment, hesitation in her expression. "I want to trust you."

My hand felt empty where hers had been. "You're right. I could be lying about this, but I'm not. I'll tell you what's going to happen. I'm heading to the transport outside, which my uncle is tracking. I'll send it off somewhere to buy you some time. You'll have an hour to get home and warn your dad. Maybe two if I can stall long enough. Don't try to warn him with a message. Virgil will intercept it in that filtering system of his." In the meantime, I had to beat my uncle to the hospital before Mom paid for my decision tonight.

"And you?"

"Let me worry about that."

She sighed. "I can't go tonight. There's something I need to do first."

"Something you *need to do*?" Bewildered, I took her hand in mine. She didn't pull away. "Legacy, you aren't listening. You have the chance to save your family here." *And yourself.*

"I'll go, just not till tomorrow. I can't help my family until I know exactly what that update does. Virgil wants me to make the big announcement tomorrow. I'll read the script in advance, find an excuse to leave the room, and escape with the information we need. That should give me several hours to get back before the update takes effect at midnight."

"Legacy. Dane could send someone else in my place. *You aren't safe here.*"

"Then I'll hide where even Virgil's cameras can't find me."

I gaped at her.

She smiled and poked my chest. "That expression right there. It's adorable. You aren't used to girls telling you no, are you?"

"This isn't a joke. I can't protect you. There's some-where I need to be tonight."

"Then take care of your business knowing that you tried. But seriously, I'll be okay. Nobody is going to kidnap me tonight." She rose onto her toes and gave me a kiss on the cheek. "Thank you."

Then she was gone.

———

I SENT the transport on a long, windy road to a distant coastal town. As it disappeared into the darkness, I turned to find Zenye marching out the front doors with two older guys, her cheeks red in the lamplight overhead.

"Hey," I said, managing a quick smile just before her fist slammed into my mouth.

My head snapped to the side. Stunned, I stumbled away and cupped my mouth as salty warmth began to flow. What in the fates?

"Bring him." She turned on her heel and marched inside, her two minions grabbing my arms and practically dragging me after her.

They shoved me into an empty meeting room full of chairs before she whirled on me. "You know you're a predictable idiot, right?"

"I . . ."

Another fist flew at me, harder this time, catching me in the jaw. I stumbled a step before the two secured me in place once more. Fates. The girl could throw a punch almost as well as Uncle Dane.

"You're going to have to enlighten me," I muttered, testing my jaw.

"I knew you'd do the stupid thing and let her go, but

your uncle didn't believe me. He likes you more than he should. Left me behind to make sure you followed through. That little performance was sweet, by the way. What a caring soul you are."

The hallway. Cameras. Virgil may have turned a blind eye to my mission tonight, but that didn't mean nobody was watching.

I groaned inwardly. I *was* an idiot.

"Do you always stalk guys you like on security cameras?" I asked with a lopsided grin. Not because it was charming but because my jaw hung at an odd angle.

This time the blow came to my solar plexus. It hit dead center, knocking the wind out of me. My breath came in gasping coughs for a good minute.

"I don't like traitors," Zenye finally said. "Liars either. So I'll give you one chance to tell me the truth about whose side you're on."

"I answer to my uncle, not you."

"You won't be answering anyone if you don't choose your words more carefully. I happily disposed of the last defector myself. His removal got a little messy, though. Do you realize how hard blood is to scrub out of white stone?"

The graffiti message Legacy had warned me about. She'd described a smear of blood. The Firebrand defector Dane had mentioned—it had to be the same guy. He was likely at the bottom of the bay right now.

"If you hurt Legacy, I'll—"

Zenye whirled around with a smirk and cut me off. "Will what? Sorry, but you'll be out of commission for a while. Perhaps a very long while." She nodded sharply to the two guys and rolled up her sleeves.

"She didn't do anything to deserve this," I shot back.

"She did nothing to deserve her privilege, either. None of the Hawkings did."

"They aren't monsters. They're just regular people who have made mistakes, and regular people can be taught. There's a more peaceful way to get change."

"What, love and hugs? Spare me the sap. Some people require a bit of remodeling before they're willing to listen. Speaking of which, we'd better get started."

The minions dragged me to a chair and forced my arms behind my back, securing them in a position that wrenched my shoulders. I endured it all with a numbness born of experience.

Legacy was in trouble. My mom was exposed at the hospital.

I'd failed.

The blows came.

TWENTY-ONE
LEGACY

I spent the night shivering in a carefully-chosen transport parked around the back of the building, thanking the fates for Travers and his universal access code.

My dreams came in bursts of memory and imagination —Firebrands breaking into my room and searching my bed, a late-night discussion with Mom about her childhood, and an argument with Dad at fourteen. Racing Alex from tree to tree when we were nine and realizing I could finally beat him. At some point Alex became Kole and we were running through the forest together, tripping on roots and getting tangled in underbrush.

After leaving Kole last night, I'd woken Millian up and filled her in while changing into a clean uniform. Now we met in the early morning shadows of the parking lot, long before either of us were usually awake. She handed me a muffin, smoothed her messy hair, and said that nobody had tried to enter our room last night. Either Kole's uncle hadn't sent anyone else after me, or they knew I wasn't there. As many times as I'd circled the building last night, I suspected the security team hadn't been able to pinpoint my exact location. A small victory, but still a victory. My heart pounded at a constant, wary rhythm.

"What time are you supposed to do this broadcast?" Millian asked, breaking off a piece of her own muffin and popping it into her mouth. Frizzy black hair fell over her face, giving her a face a wild effect.

"Two hours, but I'm not waiting. I'll march up to his office and demand to see the script so I can practice. If I don't return within thirty minutes after the broadcast, send that message to my dad like we discussed."

"I can't decide whether this plan is stupid or brave."

"The best plans are a little of both." In truth, Kole's words continued to haunt me. *I can't protect you here.* Even if Virgil and the Firebrand leader were truly working together to overthrow Dad, they kept secrets from each other. At the very least, they disagreed on how to use me. Virgil needed me for this broadcast and Kole's uncle wanted to use me for some kind of ransom. My plan to escape both and save my family would require the biggest risk of my life.

The locked wing door clicked open when I arrived. After a long walk, I reached a desk with a clerk whose eyebrows drew together in what seemed like permanent disapproval. He ushered me to Virgil's office without a word.

The office was as large and luxurious as I expected— old-fashioned leather-look sofas, a board game I doubted had ever been used set up on a heavy side table. A statue of Virgil dead center, like this was some public park. A fire extinguisher bigger than any I'd ever seen resting on the wall next to his desk. Mom's fire had really gotten to him.

A giant window covered the exterior wall, framing a massive view of the stark-white bridge jutting back to land. It was a strong reminder of how far away my family was.

The bay was a dull gray under the stormy sky. Virgil had chosen real glass for this view. It was too beautiful to be tinted in green.

I initiated the recording feature in my implant just as Director Virgil turned in his chair. It would livestream to Millian across the building.

"Miss Hawking," he said, feigning surprise. "You're early. Water packet?" He opened a small coolbox under his desk and retrieved one, holding it out to me. I shook my head. No way was I accepting food or drink from this man, sealed or not.

The victory of solving Mom's mystery was vastly over-shadowed by what this all meant. This man had looked into my mother's eyes and spouted lies. He'd planned her murder and covered up her death. Then he'd found the nerve to pretend it was an accident while stealing her research. He was every bit the criminal Dad thought, and I was about to prove it.

"I came early to read the script," I said, plopping myself onto the sofa and schooling my face to look nonchalant. "The one you were supposed to send me last night?"

"The script." He didn't look fooled. "You understand, of course, that you'll be unable to leave or communicate with anyone outside this room once you've read it. We can't allow any details to spread before they're announced."

"Sure, if that makes you feel better."

He scowled at my dismissiveness. "That includes the recording you're streaming to your friend, I'm afraid. The security room will be intercepting it now. If you don't want strangers hearing our conversation, I recommend that you discontinue the recording."

My smile slipped. Had he known from the second I walked in? I ended the recording, trying to pretend like I didn't care, and shot off a quick message to Millian. It immediately came back as undeliverable.

My heart sank further as I searched my captures and found the graffiti image gone as well. No evidence. Any accusations I made after today would be my word against Virgil's. I muttered a curse.

I was on my own.

Virgil's smile tightened. "That's better. Now, may I ask why you want to read the script?"

He thought he'd shaken me, but he was wrong. *I will not be used.* "If the words come from my mouth, I'm endorsing them. It's a reasonable request to know what I'll be saying."

"Reasonable, yes." He leaned forward. "But let me ask you something. Your father gives an average of ten public speeches a week. Do you really think the words he speaks are his own?"

"He may not write them, but he wouldn't say anything he didn't mean."

"On the contrary. You think of him as the head of a triangle, so to speak. That belief comes from a lack of understanding of our political system. The triangle is actually upside-down. Miss Hawking, your father is a face programmed by committees and representatives to deliver information. When your brother ascends, he'll do the exact same thing."

I shook my head. "That's not true." It couldn't be true. Dad wasn't perfect, but he was no puppet. "You said this was an implant announcement and nothing more. If you're trying to turn this into an anti-Hawking declaration, I won't do it."

"You won't be selling anyone out. You'll be protecting your country through a time of transition."

Country before family, country before self. A mantra I knew too well. "I want to know details right now."

Virgil sat back in his chair with a sigh. "I was right, then. You came here in an underhanded manner, intending to shake up my company."

"I couldn't care less about your company. I just want the truth for once."

"The truth? Your father points fingers, suspecting everyone, and your brother believes everything he's told. But you—you're different, aren't you? You have your mother's analytical mind."

"My analytical mind says you're avoiding my questions. Enough of this. Either give me the script or tell me what the update does that will hurt my father's position. Otherwise we're done here."

"Strong demands from a lab candidate who doesn't belong in a lab. While I'm not obligated to answer any of your questions, let me assure you that the update won't hurt your father's position. Contrary to what you may believe, I don't have that kind of political power."

"What about the Firebrands, then?" I spat, my words hot and angry. So much for playing it cool. "I know about your alliance. How could you turn against your own country?"

He chuckled. "You're as fiery as your mother was."

"The mother you killed to steal her life's research from? Yes, I am."

He nodded, not surprised in the least. "I figured you would come to that conclusion. It isn't true, but it would certainly solve all your problems, wouldn't it?"

"Not all of them." Mom still wasn't here, and nothing either of us said would bring her back.

"Then let's discuss what really happened. She and I

both knew the potential of her project, but we disagreed on how it should be used." He shrugged. "She was always a smart one. Found a loophole in the contract and made sure the project was licensed to her instead of Neuromen. By the time I discovered my oversight, she had closed the project and written it off as a failure."

"That's when you killed her."

A grimace crossed his face, combined with naked pain. It was so startling, so unexpected, that the next accusation fled my mind.

"My anger got in the way of sense," Virgil said, his voice rough. "When I suspected her plan, I chose to do nothing. I suppose that places the blame for her death squarely on my shoulders."

I rose and slammed a fist on his desk, making its contents jump. "Don't lie to me. You are *not* the victim here. You killed my mother and planned to pretend her implant update was yours all along. Now I'm here to expose you."

"Expose me?" He chuckled. "You're going to hail me as one of the greatest inventors in history, and you'll do it publicly."

I gaped. "You really think I'm still doing your stupid broadcast?"

"I know you are. The fact that you committed to spend your life in a field you care nothing about simply to investigate your mother's death proves that you care deeply for the safety of your family. This update, however, is as close to my offspring as anything will ever be. I mean to protect it no matter the cost. Your participation here today will ensure that we both get what we want."

Panic rose in my throat like bile. I swallowed it back with a grimace. "Elaborate."

"That dear grandmother of yours. She's lived at that coastal manor for, what, twenty years now?"

No. Not Gram. "Don't you hurt her."

"I have no desire to hurt her. My agents have been stationed in her house for years and have never harmed the woman. Yet."

I heard Carmen's voice in my head and thought of her irritation whenever I stopped by. The guards who weren't really guards. The medic who barely cared about her health. Were they *all* Virgil's spies?

I had to warn her.

He read my intentions immediately. "Go ahead and try. She has no implant. If she did, I would have blocked her from you too. Your determination to avoid society has resulted in a convenient lack of allies, Miss Hawking. The technology in your head is mine. You can't use it to fight me." He cocked his head. "Neurotechnology is the world now. Whoever controls the implants controls the world."

The walls were closing in, sucking the air from my lungs. I'd been completely disarmed even before my arrival here. Alex was right. Virgil had found a way to use me after all, and I'd walked right into it. Speak against my father and lose what remained of my family forever, or refuse and lose Gram. Both choices were utterly unthinkable.

"Dad would know it was you," I snapped. "Murdering his mother would only seal his anger against your company."

He waved his hand dismissively. "Your father has already lost that battle. My allies have seen to that. I'll have your answer now. Give our glorious introduction speech and I'll dismiss my agents from your grandmother's house. Reject me and she'll be dead by nightfall."

I couldn't lose Gram when I'd already lost so much. It

tore at my heart to even consider it. But I was still a Hawk-ing, and I knew my duty. I'd sworn to never be used again. It was a promise I'd made to myself. Not my country, not my family. A promise to Legacy Hawking, and one I intended to keep.

Problem was, there wasn't enough time to warn Gram. Traveling to her house would take far too long. *Fates.* There had to be a way out of this.

I made my way to the window, pretending to consider his question. The bridge several hundred meters below may as well have been on another planet. I placed my hand on the glass and marveled at how smooth it was. Odd that he'd chosen the real thing for a window so high up.

"Well?"

I glanced at his fire extinguisher and put it all together. In case of emergency, Virgil wanted an easy escape. That meant breakable glass.

It also meant a fire escape. I eased myself to the right, searching. *There.* The corner of a rail was barely visible.

Virgil stood, frowning.

I didn't think. I just lunged at the fire extinguisher, tore it from the wall, and pulled the pin.

"No!" he shrieked, but I'd already aimed it at him and pulled the handle. The pressure sent me stumbling back-ward. A couple of steps and I gained control once again. Virgil dove under his desk as white foam covered the chair where he'd just been.

Stage two. Grunting, I launched the heavy metal tin toward the window and lifted an arm to shield my eyes.

The glass shattered and came down in a sheet that looked remarkably like falling rain. The crash stabbed at my ears. Virgil screamed for his guards, but I was already taking two steps backward, measuring the window with my eyes. Jagged glass lined the edges, glittering a dare.

Then I sprinted at the opening and leaped.

"Stop that girl!" Virgil growled from somewhere behind me as I landed onto the metal landing with a painful *bang*. The fire escape was narrower than I'd imagined. Another few inches and I would have jumped clean over the walkway. I grabbed the rail to pull myself up and swung over the first few steps leading downward.

Reject me, and she'll be dead by nightfall. A sinking feeling in my stomach spurred me on. I had to find someone who could send a message to my family, and quickly. But how? I couldn't run all the way back to town before he gave his kill order. Gram would be gone long before I arrived.

I leaped the last half of the floor, flinching upon impact with the concrete, and sprinted for the parking lot.

By the sound of feet pounding on metal behind me, I could tell Virgil's guards had launched themselves out onto the fire escape as well. There would be others. I had to get away *now*.

A for-hire transport pulled up, and I dashed toward it. The passenger opened the door and stepped out just as I reached her. I dove inside and yanked the door closed, ignoring her yells of protest. "Hawking Estate!" I cried.

The vehicle beeped a warning. "Voice not authorized."

I recited Travers's override code and tried again. No luck. The woman who'd slid out began to bang on the window with her fists. A second later, the guards pulled her off and began circling the vehicle.

Maybe this wasn't a for-hire transport after all and I'd just thrown out its owner. I swore. An old memory surfaced of Dad teaching Alex a similar code. Something about Mom . . .

It came back. "Hawking Override Code Andreah 2168. Take me to Hawking Estate now!"

A click confirmed the code, and the transport began to move.

Thank you, Dad.

I plastered myself against the seat in case the guards decided to use stunners, but their shouts faded behind me as the vehicle shot over the bridge toward town.

TWENTY-TWO
LEGACY

THE TRANSPORT WAS twenty minutes out when it began to sputter.

"No, no, no," I moaned, leaning forward to look at the dashboard and telltale blinking red light. Travers kept my transport charged at all times, but this vehicle's owner obviously hadn't. Or I'd stolen it before she could.

I quickly did the math. Despite a transport's speed maximum and my tiny lead, Virgil's guards wouldn't be far behind. I had a minute, maybe two. Even if I hid, Virgil would simply pinpoint my implant location.

"Next exit," I ordered the transport, which clicked a confirmation and pulled off to the side, sputtering harder now. The remaining distance would take half a day on foot, especially while walking through a thick forest of trees to avoid being seen from the road.

I tried once more to send a message to Dad. It was rejected immediately.

Time to find another ride, and quick. Most citizens would be happy to assist Hawking's daughter. Then again, if I flagged down the wrong vehicle, I'd end up right back in Virgil's hands.

I didn't have hours to waste getting back. I didn't have minutes. If I couldn't contact Dad for help, I'd have to rely on strangers to contact him for me. Unfortunately, mine was the only vehicle parked off the road. I'd have to flag one down.

Unless there was someone Virgil hadn't thought to block from my implant list. Someone only Dad and Alex knew about.

I pulled up Travers's name and sent off a quick message. There was nothing this time. No error message, but no confirmation of arrival either. It was as if I'd sent it into thin air.

Behind me, another transport pulled off the exit. It was the generic model, a little muddy, with a catering logo on the side. Upper class but not Neuromen quality. Worth a try.

I waved my arms, walking toward the road. The vehicle slowed immediately and pulled to the side. A door opened, revealing a girl a few years younger than I was. "You okay?"

Hesitating, I looked up the road. "I'm fine. Just need a ride to . . ." I trailed off, watching a second transport follow and park right behind hers.

Three doors opened. Four figures stepped out, all wearing blue uniforms identical to mine except for the gold bar across the chest.

I cursed and turned to the girl. "Send a message to His Honorable Hawking. His mother is in danger. Tell him to hide the whole family until I can come."

She squinted at me. "I don't have that kind of access."

We were out of time. I turned my back on her and ran toward the forest. Frantic voices followed.

Four against one. Adrenaline fueled my sprint, taking me deep into the darkness of the thick treeline.

Just another track and just another race. I could almost imagine Kole running beside me, concocting ways to trick me into letting him win.

"Up there!" someone shouted behind me, and I put on another burst of speed.

The forest couldn't possibly get creepier, yet somehow, the farther I plunged in, the darker and more forlorn it grew. Before long, the sound of footsteps grew quiet in the distance. A bird squawked its anger as I flew past its perch, irritated at my determination to put as much distance between me and those guards as possible.

Then the forest grew lighter, thinner. Happier. I was gasping at this point. My ankles felt sore from running on such uneven terrain. I couldn't keep this up forever.

Another distant shout, closer this time. It felt like I'd been running for five years. There was nowhere to hide that they couldn't track me, but something inside drove me on. Giving up meant giving in to Virgil, and I couldn't do that while my family needed me.

I leaped over a root and realized my own recklessness too late. The other side dropped down in a sharp descent. I stumbled to catch my footing and felt my left ankle give way with a pop.

Pain stabbed up my leg, taking my breath with it.

I hobbled toward a tree and eased myself down onto a root, imagining my pursuers drawing closer with each second that passed. My ankle had already begun to swell. Sprained.

The voices drew closer.

I looked around for a branch, but there was nothing substantial enough to defend myself with. Not that I was in condition to do any fighting against one man right now, much less four. It was all I could do to sit and suck pained breaths through gritted teeth.

A message from Travers arrived.

I gasped and opened it, my blinking clumsy.

COAST STATION 44

There was nothing else. I read it again in disbelief. What was that supposed to mean?

Shouts. They were almost here.

I peered down the hill again to find that it wasn't a hill at all. It was a cliff. It grew rockier closer to the bottom and leveled out into sand and gravel. The coast. It was my only chance.

I started to limp my way down, clinging to trees growing stubbornly toward the sky while the ground continued to drop beneath me. With every step, my ankle throbbed as if a knife extended from the bone.

I was only halfway down when the voices reached the top of the hill. A dog barked, far too close.

My chest was aflame now. Dogs. That's how they'd stayed with me for so long. Now it was a race to the water, and I could barely walk. All I could do was keep going.

I carefully picked my way down, letting the upward curvature of the tree trunks hold my weight. My good foot slipped in the sandy soil once, but I caught myself before I plunged to the ground several dozen meters below. Halfway there now.

Heads appeared above me, and a shout rang through the forest. I was out of time.

I half slid, half stumbled down the rest of the way, my

ears straining for the slightest sound. There was talking above me, then the yelp of a dog followed by silence.

When I reached the bottom, I dared a glance upward. The dog was picking its way down, tail dragging. The poor mutt wasn't any happier about this than I was.

I took off running toward the coastline. It was more of a hop-skip-limp combination. Adrenaline combined with my body's natural painkillers were all that fueled me now. The water line was visible in the distance, a reward just beyond the rocks. The outline of a tiny building stood to the side.

The dog barked, startling me with how close it was. I cut the limp and settled into a downright sprint, awkward as it was with all the rocks and my ankle. If I made it to that tall little building, I could escape the animal and catch my breath.

As I drew closer, the structure also grew clearer. Faded red paint covered half its surface. The remains of a number took up almost the entire back side.

45.

Oh. A lifeguard station—but it was the wrong number.

I shot Travers another message and rounded the building just as the dog reached me. I leaped onto the ladder and climbed up as the dog's teeth grazed my hurt foot. I pulled my legs up beneath me and perched like a cornered squirrel as the dog began to bark.

Those guards would be descending that hill right now, if they hadn't already. I didn't have long. But my options were limited. Running would be hard enough without a hurt ankle, especially with a snapping animal after me. I could dive into the water, but I wasn't a strong swimmer even when my ankle worked. One of those men would haul me back before I swam fifty meters.

As if responding to my thought, an old-fashioned boat motor whirred in the distance, a familiar figure at its wheel.

My entire body sagged with relief. I'd know that man's lanky outline anywhere.

The dog stopped barking and began to wag its tail, looking behind the tower. The guards were nearly here.

I placed my foot onto the top rung of the ladder and leaped over the dog. The rocky sand caught me, but the landing was rough, and I collapsed. The dog was on me in an instant. It snapped at my arm, ripping the sleeve as I tore away.

"Ray, here!" one of the guards called, and the dog backed off. I didn't wait. Jumping to my feet, I hobbled for the water. There was another shout as the men realized my intentions, but the yell was quickly swallowed by the waves as I plunged in.

The salty water immediately clogged my throat, my eyes, my ears. I coughed to clear it from my lungs, but more was ready to replace it. The scratches from that blasted dog's claws burned. I kept moving forward, the whirr of the boat motor louder than the gentle roar of the waves. *Swim.*

My arms moved out of desperation more than anything. Swimming blind, I scrambled toward the sound. Suddenly the motor cut off, and I felt a hand grab the back of my shirt. A grunt, then a second hand reaching gently around my waist. I placed my hands on the side of the boat and kicked to launch myself up.

Then I was inside, dripping water all over carpet far too nice for a boat.

Travers shook his head in disbelief. "You're bloody crazy."

"You're right on time, as always." I wiped my eyes on

my arms, but it didn't help much. The figures on the beach stood in a huddle, sending the occasional glance my direction. They'd be requesting a boat to follow us. "Shall we go for a ride?"

He chuckled. "Yes, ma'am."

TWENTY-THREE
LEGACY

As we rounded the coastline of Old Town and headed for a rougher part of the shore, Travers agreed to send a message to Dad but shook his head about Gram. "She's fine. I'm taking you to her."

I stared at him. "You mean the spies are gone?"

"I mean she got away."

Fates. The relief came with a wave of exhaustion even stronger than my pain, but now I had a dozen questions. "Did you get her out? How did you know to do that? I didn't even know you owned a boat."

"I don't. This one belongs to your family. You'd be surprised what the Hawkings have stored away. And I didn't get your grandmother out, exactly. More like the other way around. Your father reassigned me to her after your abrupt departure. Last night, she insisted we go for a drive before dawn and swore me to secrecy. The woman brought along no less than ten blankets." He chuckled. "By the time we reached the storage warehouse, I had your grandmother's plan all figured out."

It wasn't until we rounded the rocks into a calmer

harbor that I understood. Gram stood there with a smile, a thin jacket pulled tight around her bony frame. Relief nearly doubled me over, and soon I was in her arms, my sprained ankle forgotten.

"They were going to hurt you," I whispered against her faded brown hair.

She patted my back. "I still have a few tricks in me. Heard them discussing their plans yesterday while they thought I was napping. Palmed my sleeping pill last night and escaped while Carmen snored away on the couch. I bet she woke up very confused." She pulled away and winked. I just laughed.

Gram led the way to a cavern I'd never noticed before, her footing sure as anything. She picked her way between the boulders like she'd done this a hundred times. Maybe she had. It was a guilty reminder that I didn't know as much about her as I assumed. I slipped twice on mud and foam while limping along behind. Travers secured the boat in a hidden cleft of rock and followed.

A warm glow from deep within the cavern cast haunting shadows of our approach. Soon we reached a small room carved out of rock. The walls were smooth and round, as if formed by the passage of a giant snake. I touched the walls and felt a thin powder on my fingers. A manmade cave?

But it was more than that, I realized as I looked around. A bedroom, complete with bed, quilt, bed stand, and a pile of books. Real, old-fashioned books. Next to the pile lay our source of light. It wasn't a lantern but rather some kind of lighted bag with tiny round pellets inside. I'd never seen the likes of it.

"Can I touch it?" I reverently asked Gram.

"Of course. One of my last bags. We intended to

produce more when we arrived all those decades ago, but the underground settlers couldn't find the ingredients they needed here. We switched to lanterns until electricity could be generated."

She sounded sad. I tried to imagine her as a teenager, a girl with a birthright and a determination to save those who looked to her for salvation. How many people had she lost along the way? How many of her friends remained?

I touched her arm. "It looks like you've spent a lot of time down here."

"Vance and I used to come here all the time, especially when the press started following us around. It was the only place we could be alone together without being tracked."

I felt my eyes widen. *Tracked.* "Gram, Virgil will find me here."

"No, he won't. This is a dead spot on the coast. Your signal would have disappeared over ten minutes ago. It's one reason I built this here—the rocky cliffs form a natural barrier from location sensors. Neither of us had implants, but Vance was always a cautious person. Malachite learned to walk right by that chair." Her face glowed. "Vance grinned from ear to ear for hours afterward. You'd have thought our son invented flight."

I pictured my father as a toddler, struggling to find footing on this dirty and uneven floor, and grinned. "Does Dad know about this place?"

"I'm sure he has memories of it, but I doubt he even recalls where it is."

Hopefully he would get Travers' message and get himself and Alex to safety. If Kole was right about the Firebrands taking over the Block, there would be bloodshed. That I knew to be true.

I glanced at the bag again. "Who were the underground settlers?"

"Oh, Legacy. I haven't spent nearly enough time with you. Shame on me."

I didn't know how to respond to that. No amount of time together would have been enough to fill the hole in my chest that Mom left behind. Now that she and Grandpa Vance were gone, we'd both felt the shift like changes in the wind.

She laughed at my expression and gestured to a pair of soft chairs in the corner. "Let's talk. We have some catching up to do."

GRAM'S STORY took most of an hour. Travers stood by the entrance of the room like a guard, though he was clearly interested in our conversation. By the time she finished, Travers and I were both staring at her. Their exodus from old NORA and creation of a new society was far more intricate and difficult than I'd imagined, and Travers had experienced it all as a child.

"Three groups of people," I muttered. "Underground settlers, the outsiders, and citizens—none of which trusted anyone else. Yet somehow you got them to work together for survival."

"The second part was easier than the first," Gram admitted with a smile. "My eventual marriage to Vance cemented two of those groups, and the third grew to trust me in time. If not for that, we would have fragmented upon our arrival."

It felt as if Gram had placed new lenses into my eyes. Everything was so much clearer now—why she'd chosen to avoid implants altogether, why she'd spent so much time at the Copper Office. The reason behind her new system and its freedoms.

"You never said what you and Dad fought about last year," I said carefully. "Did you disagree about politics?"

Some of the light in her eyes faded. "We've always disagreed about politics. I would have been concerned if he didn't. He leads the country now, not me. I created a foundation, and he's built upon it as he saw fit."

She'd effectively dodged the question. I looked at Travers, who had a hint of displeasure in his expression. He didn't understand why I would pursue this when it made Gram uncomfortable. "Then why? What disagreement is terrible enough to make you avoid each other?"

"Avoid?" She shook her head. "I've invited him to visit me nearly every week in the past few months. Even stopped by your home a few times. He wouldn't see me."

"Because he's angry at something you did?"

She swallowed. "Because he's angry at something I *allowed*. Even though I had no idea what the consequences would be at the time. Believe me, I've suffered for it every day since."

Gram had a lot of sorrows, but one in particular seemed to haunt her. "Grandpa Vance's death."

"Before DNR-6 was discovered and officially named, dozens of patients were getting sick with a strange brain disease. Vance's sister was one of the first to fall ill."

"Aunt Lucy," I said softly. She'd died of the disease just weeks before Grandpa Vance. Since Aunt Laura was long gone, it made her his last remaining family member.

She nodded. "Vance was never an emotional man, but his sister's illness nearly broke him. The physicians offered an experimental medication. Vance was reluctant to try it, given Lucy's weak state. He concocted a plan to get himself infected. If it worked, he would allow the physicians to use the treatment on himself to see if it would save his sister. He grew obsessed with the idea. It was all he would talk about." Gram's voice wobbled, and she blew out a quick breath to gain control of her emotions. "What was I supposed to do? Say he couldn't try to save someone he desperately loved? No matter how much I needed him, I had no right to say no."

To my surprise, Travers broke in. "Lucy Hawking was the first to be placed in a medical coma to try and stop the advancement of the disease."

"And it worked for a while," Gram said. "Vance was hopeful. Everything went according to plan—the implantation, everything. They infected him with the virus from his own sister's brain. Then they put him through the treatment. When that failed, they tried another and another."

This I remembered. The bottles of medicines next to my grandfather's bed. The constant flow of IVs and medics. The press camped outside their manor for news of his progress. His face growing lean, gaunt, and finally paperlike as his body rejected the nutrients the medics offered.

Gram fell silent. She didn't have to tell me what happened next. Rather than saving the siblings, we lost them both within weeks of each other. Gram must have admitted the truth to Dad the night they'd fought.

Being angry at Gram meant Dad didn't have to deal with the fact that his own father had taken the biggest gamble of his life and lost.

"I've often wondered what drove me to agree to his plan," Gram said. "Was it the worry that he would resent me for letting his sister die? Did I go along with it simply because I was too weak to do otherwise? Or did I love him enough to let him do what he felt was right, no matter the consequence? I don't blame Malachite at all for his feelings, Legacy. He's lost so much."

Now he was about to lose the Copper Office too, at the very least. I felt sick. Here we sat discussing Gram's life story, and Virgil would be releasing a dangerous update into the world in just a few hours.

Something tickled my mind. "Wait. You said they extracted the virus from Aunt Lucy and placed it in Grandpa Vance. How did that work?"

She looked surprised at the change of subject. "They couldn't get the virus to transmit through the air. It had to be injected into his bloodstream before it could take effect."

"But Aunt Laura didn't have it injected, so how did she catch it?"

Gram frowned. "I'm not sure. We never determined that."

"Hundreds of patients have caught it in the past few years. Did they ever look for similarities in their situations? Jobs? Family? Blood type?"

"Yes, actually. Medics were surprised to find that most of the victims came from higher-profile families. There have been victims from the Shadows, but the majority are children from wealthier parents. They looked into it and eventually assumed it was nothing more than a concerning environmental factor. Rather than making an announcement and creating a nationwide panic that wouldn't solve anything, we poured national funds into medical research and built new hospitals to accommodate the sick."

I rose to my feet and began to pace. "Maybe it isn't environmental. Maybe the common factor isn't where they live or work at all. Did all of the victims have implants?"

Gram's eyes narrowed. "Yes, now that I think about it. All except Vance."

I paused and looked at both Gram and Travers in turn. "What if the disease technically isn't a disease at all? It may look like brain sickness, but I wouldn't be surprised if Virgil discovered how to trigger symptoms in specific individuals —and if Mom resisted him."

Gram swore under her breath. It sounded more like Grandpa Vance than herself, and I couldn't decide whether to laugh or grimace.

"I don't understand," Travers said. "What are you saying exactly?"

"This update he's about to roll out—I think some have already received it." My voice grew surer with each word. "Every death has occurred in the past two years, right? He must have been triggering the disease as a test. Now he's about to update everyone. He'll be able to pick and choose who he wants to get sick." Starting with the Hawking family. Only Gram would be spared.

Virgil had said the update wouldn't hurt Dad's position. He hadn't said anything about the update not hurting *Dad*.

The blood drained from Travers's face. "Fates."

Gram looked ashen. "My spies reported there was a line of Firebrands giving blood today at the hospital. Could that be linked somehow?"

I thought about Virgil's blood draw requirement. A coincidence? I just didn't see how the pieces fit together, no matter how hard I shoved. "I'm not sure."

"It's safe to assume the Firebrands and their supporters will be spared while others suffer," Gram said. "By the time the infected begin to die or overcome the disease, it will be too late. Our country will be in chaos."

"And the Firebrands will step in, find a 'cure,' and put

the country under emergency law. We can bet that law will lead eventually to reinstating the Rating system. They'll ensure that their own scores are higher than everyone else to remain in power." I frowned. "It's brilliant, but there's a piece missing. What does Virgil get out of this? He can't expect the citizens to overlook the fact that all this originated with an implant update. Everyone will know Neuromen had something to do with it."

"Maybe that's the plan?" Gram suggested. "The Firebrands will seem like saints after that. They'll put one of their own on the throne and then pardon him."

I shook my head. "I'm not convinced the Firebrands will ascend right away. If they're smart, they will have placed someone in the Block long before now to succeed Dad. Someone the people already trust, a transition figure until they're ready to take control." Most likely a member of Dad's cabinet. He'd long suspected the Firebrands had infiltrated the group.

Gram and Travers were silent for a long moment, digesting the information.

"Can people be instructed on how to remove their implants?" Travers finally asked.

Gram shook her head. "They can only be removed surgically. Some people have died even under trained hands. Neurotechnology is complicated."

"Then we need to stop that update from going out in the first place," I said firmly. "Gram, will the military come if you call? We can send an army into the lab to stop things and arrest Virgil."

She shook her head sadly. "Most of our troops are fighting in border skirmishes with Malrain. By the time we gathered a group substantial enough to penetrate Virgil's security, it would be too late."

He would be expecting that anyway. Virgil's lab would be more secure than a military base right now. Only his own people would be allowed to come and go. I couldn't walk in through the front doors, maybe, but I did have an advantage others didn't.

Until this morning, it had been my home.

My idea was risky, but Grandpa Vance's plan, failed as it was, gave me a boldness that echoed from my blood. Hawkings took care of each other.

I checked the time. Another two hours until sunset. Unless Virgil changed his plans, the update would launch at midnight. "Travers, has Dad responded yet?"

He shook his head.

"Then we'll have to do this alone." I looked at them both, and they met my gaze with a steady one of their own.

Gram wore a stern look. "You're in no condition to storm Neuromen, Legacy. Much less by yourself."

"I have a friend who can sneak me in." Assuming Millian was okay. I worried that Virgil knew she'd helped me. "The less people involved, the more likely we'll make it."

Her lips pursed. "I'll send Travers with you, but we'll wait until darkness falls. If he thinks it can't be done, you'll return immediately. In the meantime, Travers, I need you to venture out and send a message to my spies. I worry that we haven't heard from Malachite yet."

Travers gave me a tight smile. "Yes, Your Honor. It would be my pleasure."

TWENTY-FOUR

KOLE

THE ADS on the wall were the first indication I was most definitely not at Neuromen. The heavy sanitizer smell was the second.

I sat bolt upright and immediately groaned. I was in a hard hospital chair, my left wrist chained to one chair arm. Every cell in my body hurt. Simply *breathing* hurt.

Everything came back. Zenye. Her thugs. *Legacy.* Was she all right?

None of this made sense. I should have been at the bottom of the bay with that Firebrand deserter, not in a hospital room bound to a chair. A chair, not a bed?

I frowned, examining my seat once again and taking silent inventory of my injuries. Breathing deep felt uncomfortable, painful, but not excruciating. Bruised ribs, then. My eyes felt swollen, and my jaw still hung unnaturally. Thankfully, my legs still seemed to work fine. I'd experienced worse.

A tiny beep sounded from across the room, and I realized I wasn't alone. A figure lay in a bed, her familiar brown hair splayed across the pillow.

Forgetting my bonds, I tried to stand and groaned as the pain hit. *Mom.* They'd moved her to a different hospital room, but it was definitely her. A beep sounded from the machine next to her head, its four glass screens indicating various readings. Her chest gently rose and fell in sleep. She was still alive. Just as important, she was still plugged in. Disconnecting her meant ending the coma, pulling her back to consciousness, and allowing the disease to complete its final stages. From previous patients' experiences, I knew that wouldn't take long.

Dane was behind this. He'd sent me here as a reminder of what he could take from me. I had to free myself and get Mom out before he arrived—a tricky feat considering I had to bring that blasted machine with me. But medical professionals did it all the time. It had to be possible.

I tested the chain at my wrist to find it was secure and tried to rock the chair instead. Too heavy and painful to boot.

"Hello," I called toward the open door, hoping a medic would hear. No answer.

Just then, a message lit up my implant screen, and my bonds were forgotten.

NEUROMEN SPECIAL UPDATE TO FOLLOW

Virgil's announcement.

I froze, watching to see if Legacy's face would appear. But the screen opened to show Virgil sitting in a dark-blue chair, wearing a suit and smiling. Next to him sat a famous announcer I recognized from the top broadcasting station. With all the makeup and hair gel and blinding white teeth, he looked like a plastic doll.

"We have a treat for you today," the announcer said. "We're here at Neuromen Labs for an official announcement, which will be made by our nation's most recognizable neurotechnological specialist. How are you, Director Virgil?"

"I'm doing remarkably well, thank you. Excited to be here today."

I looked past him and scanned the room, which had to be Virgil's office considering the statue of himself in the center. Humble guy. Legacy was nowhere to be found.

The announcer looked overly interested. "Neuromen has been tight-lipped about its latest project in past months. Why the secrecy?"

"I'd prefer to use the word 'caution.' We didn't want anyone experimenting with the technology and hurting themselves while we worked out any potential issues. But I'm proud to stand behind this particular update. It's like nothing we've released before."

"We're excited to hear details," the announcer said. "But first, you've expressed regret in the past about not being able to offer updates to those in lower income levels. Tell us how this one will affect them."

Virgil's eyes gleamed. He'd written this speech, no doubt, and placed this question here intentionally. Money and rising costs were a favorite argument among Firebrands and the lower classes.

"For the first time in history, Neuromen's latest implant update will be available to everyone at no cost. It fixes previous issues and brings everyone to the same level of technology regardless of station. It's something I should have done long ago. I apologize for not taking the initiative in previous versions, but as the lab's director, I'm also its chief financial manager. Bills need to be paid."

"That's an impressive announcement, considering how expensive previous updates have been. How will this affect Neuromen Labs?"

"We have a financial reserve we hope will carry us through until future projects are announced."

I cursed at the brilliance of it. Virgil's strategy was clearly aimed at dethroning Hawking. By helping the lower classes, he became the benefactor Hawking wasn't. Even Dane wouldn't have anticipated this.

"Will that financial reserve protect the lab from Hawking's legal charges?" the blond man asked.

Virgil sighed and leaned back in his chair, suddenly looking like an old man. "I don't blame Hawking's personal feelings toward me after the unfortunate accident that took his wife. But I will say that his accusations are unfounded and, frankly, damaging to our country's progress. I also think his laws were written to give certain businesses a stranglehold on the industry. It's one reason I feel strongly about offering this update to everyone. I hope Hawking sees our vision rather than trying again to close us down."

Another cunning move—labeling Hawking as emotional and unreasonable.

For the first time, I wondered how much Legacy's father knew. He seemed to be the only man standing up to Virgil. Was it truly revenge for his wife's death, or did he know this update would threaten his country?

The announcer still looked weirdly happy. I suspected he'd wear the same expression even discussing war or mass murder. "The number of activists calling for restructuring rises by the year. Electricity mandates, employment restrictions, and retail laws hurting small businesses are major factors in their complaints. How do you feel this will influence their cause?"

"They have a point. Other growing nations don't have rolling blackouts, especially not in the slums. They focus their efforts on creating jobs and encouraging upward growth, not placing people in bad situations from which they can't escape. I certainly wish the Hawkings would see that our new system is far less effective than the old, but sadly, that doesn't seem likely. All I can do is my part to help." He gazed right into the camera now. His meaning was clear. *I can't unseat Hawking, but the people can.*

I was wrong. Virgil hadn't written this speech alone. The subtlety was clearly Virgil's, but the strength of it—the *punch*—was definitely Dane's. The two had to have written it together the other night.

The announcer nodded. "A lot of thought must have gone into this new project. It sounds like an incredible opportunity for the nation if we can pull together and fight for our potential."

Fight. A carefully chosen word that could be viewed different ways. This speech would serve as Virgil and Dane's rallying cry without giving Hawking any legal grounds for arrest.

"When will this update take effect?" the announcer asked.

"Assuming Hawking doesn't show up on my doorstep in his pajamas with an army of enforcers? Tonight at midnight." The two laughed at the idea, but the point was clear. They quickly closed the interview.

I sat back in my chair, heart pounding. Virgil hadn't given his usual purchase instructions, but that wasn't out of kindness. This was a mandatory update. Everyone would receive it whether they wanted it or not. Even Hawking.

A big question remained. Where was Legacy?

I scrolled through the news feeds and grimaced. Announcers seemed excited about the speech. Within minutes, people were already swarming the Block with protests, demanding Hawking drop the charges against

Neuromen. Witnesses said Hawking was still inside. He had to be sweating through his suit by now, facing such a rapidly growing crowd after a speech like that. There was no mention about Legacy on any of the stations.

I dismissed the feed and sat there, staring at the wall. The Firebrands were about to get exactly what we wanted. I should have been happy about it.

The sickness in my gut said otherwise.

I rotated my wrist, examining the chain again. The metal had to be stronger than a chair molded from reinforced plastic. Time to be smart about this. Another look revealed the chair legs were bolted to the floor. The chair wouldn't rock from side to side, but it squeaked a tiny bit when I leaned forward. It would have to be enough.

I spent several minutes wrenching my body forward, each thrust tearing at my wrist and irritating my already sore rib cage. Just when I was about to admit defeat, the squeak turned into a metallic groan and one chair leg came free. Since I hadn't expected it, I rolled and hit the floor, my wrist still chained and extended at an awkward angle. The chair now sat crooked.

Rising quickly, I pushed aside the pain and went to work on the other side. A minute later, it came free. I was now the proud owner of a heavy hospital chair.

I hurried to Mom's bedside, pulling the chair along behind me. She looked so peaceful. If only we could talk without it risking her life. They said the machine could sustain her for up to three years while science created a cure for the disease. I just had to buy us more time.

Shoving the brake up on the wheels beneath her bed, I gave it an experimental shove. Not too bad. The machine, however, needed to be switched to its battery before I moved it anywhere. Then I had to bribe a medic to help push the—

"Nice chair," Dane said from the doorway.

I gritted my teeth and turned slowly toward him. "Let's cut the dramatics and discuss this."

"There's been enough talk. It's time for showing. I wanted you to see what happens when a Firebrand shuns his oath."

I placed myself between him and my mother, my heart seizing in a way I hadn't experienced since my childhood beatings. "Then show me. Leave an innocent woman out of it."

Dane stepped inside, allowing me to see that he wasn't alone. Zenye's two grunts moved to take Dane's place in the doorway, then turned to face the hall. I was trapped.

"You make this so easy," Dane said, his gaze flicking to Mom. I stepped sideways to block his view. "Anyone else would have realized their mother was dying anyway, but you cling to her like a good little son."

"She isn't dying. They're looking for a cure."

"She was always going to die. No DNR-6 patient has ever survived. Your hope is admirable, but if you look closer, you'll see it was all in vain. The coma is simply another ploy by the medics to take an honest worker's money." He stopped his advance, standing right next to me now.

I refused to accept his words. But the longer I looked at Mom, the more I saw. Her blue-tinged lips and fingernails. The darkness surrounding her closed eyes. Her white skin, drained of its usual life, her barely moving chest. None of that had been there last week.

Dane turned away in disgust. "Guards, secure him. Do a better job this time."

I stiffened, but there was nowhere to retreat as the two

advanced. This time, I was ready when they reached me. I swung, connecting with a face while the second dove in. His arm reached around my shoulders to hold me back. I slipped my foot behind his and let him fall. He landed with a grunt, his shoulder narrowly missing the cords connecting Mom's machine to its power box in the wall. Too close.

It distracted me long enough for the other to land a punch at my already-sore solar plexus. I cried out as the pain nearly buckled my knees. Within seconds, they'd dragged me from Mom's bed back to the corner again, one hand on each shoulder. I tried to wrench away and got an elbow to the temple for my trouble.

"I hope that girl was worth it," Dane said, bending over to disconnect the cord.

"Don't!" I cried.

"Too late." He lifted the plug for me to see, dangling between his fingers, and tossed it aside. A high-pitched shriek sounded from the machine. All four screens read EMERGENCY. "I should have done that long ago. Maybe you would have been less distracted. Then again, maybe not."

Pain drilled a rhythmic hole in my chest where my heart should be. *Not like this.* "Please."

He stalked toward me, his expression murderous. "Now my brother's son begs. Tell me. Did you stop when my brother begged for mercy?"

Now my heart threatened to stop altogether. The room lurched to the side, and I struggled to steady myself. "What?"

"Don't play stupid. I'm asking if you gave my brother any mercy before you killed him."

I glanced at Mom, trying to make sense of all this. "I—I didn't—"

The blow came so hard I felt my neck snap. The floor leaped toward me, but the guards at either side managed to right me before I met it. Pain like I'd never experienced ignited in my face.

Dane wasn't drunk today. That made him infinitely more dangerous.

"Virgil has street footage of you dragging your father's body down the street that night," he said, his face contorted in rage. "You left him by a dumpster for children to find. Didn't even have the courage to dispose of him yourself."

My tone was stronger than expected. "I'd do it again if it meant protecting Mom."

Dane's eyes narrowed sharply. He clasped and unclasped his fists, looking deadly calm. I knew that look well. It was the same expression Dad had worn when he thought Mom needed to be taught her place. The look of a murder about to happen.

He reached into his pocket and pulled out a knife.

Hands tightened on my shoulders.

My breath caught.

A realization made me straighten slowly. Even if I died today, my uncle's anger still lay upon me and not Mom. There was still a chance some frantic medic would hear the machine's alarm and plug her back in. Still a chance they were wrong about her pulling out of the coma too fast.

Still a chance . . .

His jaw flexed, then he turned to Mom.

I felt my eyes go round. *No.* I tried to lunge, but the guards yanked me back.

My uncle plunged the blade deep into Mom's chest.

A cry tore from my soul. "No!"

Mom's entire body rocked. She sucked in a quick breath, her eyes flying open in shock. She searched the room as her torso convulsed, struggling for oxygen that would not be found. Her panicked gaze found mine.

Then the panic faded. All that remained was a strange peace. Her eyes flicked to my guards and then my uncle's face before returning to mine again. There was understanding there. She knew I was trying to break free of my father's shadow.

She approved.

Then the breath escaped her lips in a long, quiet sigh.

I grunted and threw myself against the guards' hold. Voices from the hallway blended with my uncle's next words, making little sense in the thickness of the moment. All I could see and hear was the stillness of my mother's body and those forever lifeless eyes.

Dane must have ordered me released because there was a tugging sensation at my wrist and then a shove from behind. I stumbled toward Mom. No matter how I blinked the warmth of my swimming eyes away, the blade remained lodged in her stilled chest. A presence moved to my side.

"My brother for your dear mommy," Dane said. He slapped my shoulder with one firm hand. "I'd kill you too, but Virgil has something special planned for you. Apparently it's difficult to find good research subjects these days." He nodded to the guards, who'd resumed their places, and headed for the door.

"Where's Legacy?" I asked, my voice flat and lifeless.

He paused in the doorway, his massive shoulders taut. He didn't turn around to look me in the eye. "She'll be handled very soon. I hope they find you a decent dumpster, nephew. You have five minutes to say goodbye." Then he was gone.

His taunt slid right off me. I stared at my mother in silence, my heart full of apologies that she would never hear.

I tucked Mom's hands next to her body and smoothed her hair before yanking the cursed blade out and tossing it into the sink. The very act made my stomach lurch. Then I pulled the sheet over her head, tucked it around her still form, and stepped back.

I'd managed to protect her from one brother but not the other. In trying to save both Mom and Legacy, I'd managed to lose both. I was neither Firebrand nor free, ally nor enemy.

Only the fates knew what I was anymore.

Maybe that was the only light in all this darkness. Now I had the power to decide, guards or no guards. As I considered my options, everything unimportant faded away until all that remained was a girl with a long, dark brown ponytail and intense green eyes.

Saving Legacy would no longer mean betrayal—it would mean breaking free of Dane once and for all. It would mean finishing what Mom and I had started together, even if that meant doing it alone.

A gasp sounded from the door, followed by a scuffle. The guards wrestled a medic back from the doorway. By the color draining from his face, the man had made a very incorrect assumption about my presence here.

"Terrorists!" he spat, and hurried out of sight. His shouts echoed down the hall after him.

"Your goodbyes are over," the taller guard said, grabbing my arm and dragging me out. I sent Mom's form a quick glance before they pulled me out of sight.

An alarm penetrated the numbness of my mind. The guards shoved me through the wide hallway toward the double doors leading outside toward the train station. Most passerby took one look at the bulky guards and threw themselves out of our way. Others saw the colorful swelling on my face and slowed, trying to ascertain what was happening. I wore my Neuromen uniform, not a hospital gown, but I certainly looked like a patient.

That gave me an idea.

A group of six security guards dressed in black uniforms rounded the building as we entered the parking lot. The train station lay just beyond.

"Help!" I shouted over my shoulder. "Firebrand kidnappers!"

They looked at each other and began to run.

My guards cursed. One backhanded me across the face and pulled us all into a slow jog. They couldn't hold my arms and run very quickly. Exactly as I'd hoped.

The guards behind us rose a shout. "Stop or you'll be stunned!" one called out.

The man holding my right arm pulled us all to a stop and turned. "Go away. This is Firebrand business."

"Release the patient so we can question him," a woman in the middle of the pack snapped, sweeping her stunner from one offender to the other. "*Now!*"

I shook free of the guards' hands and gave my shoulders a roll, thinking quickly and ignoring the pinching sensation in my rib cage. "I woke up to find these guys dragging me out of my hospital bed. They say I owe them money or something."

It was the right thing to say. A Firebrand had snuck inside the hospital a few years ago and beaten a patient nearly to death. It wasn't upon Dane's order, but we'd been forced to lie low for a while. The hospital guards' eyes narrowed and leveled on the thugs once more.

"Thanks for the help," I said, sending the hospital guards a quick salute. Then I bolted.

"Hey!" the woman called, but she didn't shoot. It would

be against hospital protocol to stun a patient unless they were under psychological treatment. By the time she searched hospital records and found my lie, I'd be long gone.

Dane's thugs—or were they Zenye's?—threw themselves into a sprint after me, but as I'd suspected, they began panting and pulled back almost immediately. Their strength was in bulk and fighting, not distance running. I let my legs fall into a natural rhythm, focusing on my breathing and refusing to acknowledge the pain in my ribs and the headache threatening to tear my head apart.

Legacy needed me—and I was pretty sure I knew where to find her.

TWENTY-FIVE

LEGACY

An incoming message startled me awake. A sharp pain in my neck meant I'd fallen asleep in the chair. Gram dozed in the bed, her bagged light bathing half her face in light. Travers sat near the entrance to our cavern, too still to be awake.

I pulled the message up quickly, but it wasn't from Dad. It was from Alex.

MEET ME AT THE BLOCK IN ONE HOUR.

I frowned. Hadn't Virgil said Alex was blocked from communicating with me? Maybe the restrictions only worked one way. But why wouldn't Dad contact me if he could? And why would he tell Alex to request a meeting at the Block after we'd specifically warned him away from there?

A second message came through. It was only one word long.

PLEASE.

My suspicions calmed. Idiot or not, Alex was still my brother. Maybe he and Dad were stuck inside the Block and needed a safe escape or something. I didn't dare reply to ask. If Alex could reach me here, maybe the location sensors could as well. I wouldn't be the one to draw Virgil upon us.

I woke Travers, who hurried away to get the boat ready. It would take almost the full hour just to get there. Then I turned to Gram, who'd rolled over to place her back toward me. I hated to leave her here alone, but this cavern was far safer than where I was about to venture. I would send Travers back to check on her.

The ride to the common docks was a choppy one. Travers took it slow, carefully picking his way through the waves. My ankle felt a little better after some rest, but it was still stiff enough to make walking painful. I gripped the seat beneath me with both hands and endured the heavy bouncing of our watercraft.

"Thank you for saving me earlier," I told Travers. "I know it's your job to drive me around, but that was definitely beyond your job description."

"As lively as your grandmother is, I do miss your after-school stories. Besides, I'm out of romance novels." He winked. "I'm happy to be your escort for the evening's events."

That was an interesting way to put it. First, rescue Dad and Alex. Second, break into the lab and stop an apocalypse. The second item of business made the first sound almost simple.

We reached the dock, climbed into my usual transport—which still smelled like Gram's hair powder—and headed for the Block.

I KNEW the instant I arrived that something was off. The earlier protestors were gone. Guards stood in their usual positions, but although they wore the same uniforms, their faces were different. Saja at the main desk with her jar full of caramel candies was gone, replaced by a stern-faced man with shaggy brown hair who watched our every step. Even the lift operator was some woman I'd never seen before, wearing a uniform that was obviously too large. She avoided my gaze as we ascended to the eighth floor, where the Copper Office was situated.

Travers and I exchanged a worried glance. If only Gram had a stunner we could have brought along. Had something happened to Alex?

Where was Dad?

We finally arrived and allowed ourselves to be ushered through the waiting room that serviced Dad's office. I shot the tiny fish in its aquarium a glance only for my breath to catch. He was there, but he floated too still and near the water's surface. As I squinted at him, I realized his belly was exposed to the sky.

The stamped copper glinting on the walls of Dad's office caught my attention first, as it always did. A family capture from two years ago graced the main wall, under which sat a glass desk that sharply contrasted with the room's classical architecture and decor. Guards lined two entire walls. They closed the door immediately after our entrance and took their places once again, stiff and solemn. Alex sat at the desk with his hands folded, his knee bouncing underneath.

"Where's Dad?" I asked immediately. Alex wore his usual uniform, but there was something different about him now. A brightness to his eyes that contrasted with the strain pulling his mouth downward. *Bad news.*

"He's safe," Alex said evenly.

Something wasn't right. There was guilt in my brother's eyes. "Alex. What do you mean by *safe?*"

"I know exactly where Dad is, and I'll take you to him soon. Patience. You never did understand how busy things can get around here, did you? Never had any interest in how a country is run or how to please important people. You scoffed at all of it."

I felt sick. "That's not true. I respect what you and Dad are doing here."

"And you're content to let us keep doing it because you're above such things."

I frowned at Travers, who watched Alex with a tight jaw. My brother went off on things sometimes, but now he looked almost manic. "What is this about?"

"It's about you knowing where you belong. I'm trying to figure out whether you do."

I took a few steps toward him. As he rose to meet me, a few of the nearest guards stiffened, ready to leap. I slowed with a sinking sensation in my stomach. They weren't here to protect us.

They were here to protect Alex.

Oh, fates. I'd been so, so stupid.

"It's you," I said softly. "You're the mole who's taking power during the transition."

"What transition? I was always next in line. Yet you're the one everyone likes. Did you know that you have three times more media coverage than I do? I'm making decisions that shape the fate of countries while the press scrambles over each other to hear how your latest haircut went."

I flushed. "I never wanted any of that."

"Your standoffish act just makes them seek you out harder. I'm tired of it."

I banged my hand on the desk, startling the tense guards. "Alex. What have you done?"

"Dad doesn't know everything. All right? He thinks he does, but he acts out of instinct and fear. I had to act to stave off a revolution and keep the Copper Office in the family. I'm doing all of us a favor."

"By locking Dad up and handing the country over to terrorists? How is that helpful to anyone?"

"See, your reaction just proves you would have driven our entire family to ruin. The Firebrands would have taken over within the week. Dad was wrong to pick you, just like he was wrong about everything else. At least this way a Hawking will still rule."

His words finally sunk in. "You mean . . . Dad wanted to name *me* his successor?"

Alex scowled and plopped down into his chair. *Dad's* chair. "I found the speech in his storage files. He wrote it a year ago even though our birthday isn't for six more months. He never said a word about it. Not when I worked for him and you lounged at home, or when you ditched the family for that stupid lab job. I deleted the speech, so nobody will ever know."

I was speechless. Why would Dad choose me over Alex?

"Even if he had announced it, though, it would be me sitting here anyway. You know why?" He leaned forward. "I pulled up your birth records and found a little discrepancy."

My stomach turned to ice. I couldn't move my feet.

The memory returned. As always, the faces were hazy against the background of toys in the playroom. I remembered only the voices. Gram's was steady, while Mom's was broken, a staccato version of her own.

The words they shared were unfamiliar. *Birth records. DNA. Features.*

Birth parents.

My reply tore free one strained, ragged layer at a time. "What discrepancy?"

"The blood sample they took at your birth. It's a girl with Hawking blood and DNA, but it isn't yours—is it, dear sister?"

I lifted my chin in defiance. "We have the same parents."

"Parents who lied to us both. Dad even admitted he never intended to tell me the truth. If he'd lie about a stranger living in my house, what else has he lied about?"

"So what if they adopted me," I said quickly, glancing at Travers. His face was unreadable. "That shouldn't matter. I'm still a Hawking."

"I don't think the people will agree. Gram's bloodline law was pretty clear. You don't carry Hawking blood, you aren't eligible to rule. I bet you were dumped off by some Shadows teenager who couldn't afford her own hospital bills, much less yours."

"I never wanted to rule, and you're still my brother. This changes nothing."

"It does if I tell everyone the truth."

The threat hovered around the chandelier above us before fading to nothing. Alex watched me expectantly. I felt Travers's eyes on my back and the accusing glares of two dozen guards. I had avoided Virgil's blood draw and the truth about my birth, but now I had to face it. A phantom nightmare from my childhood was now becoming irrevocably real. If I wasn't a Hawking, what was I?

The threat was clear. Expose Alex as a traitor, and I'd

lose everything I was. As much as I hated the spotlight, I'd grown used to the warmth.

My brother bared his teeth. "Here's your choice. Support me and you can go back to that lab and live your life. Fight me and I'll expose you as the fraud you are. Neither option gets you the throne like Dad wanted, but we both know the right Hawking is in place."

"People will die if you let this update happen," I snapped. "They trust us for protection."

"The Firebrands' ideas are a little extreme, maybe, but NORA survived for almost a hundred years under the Rating system. In case you didn't notice, ours isn't doing so great either. It may be worth a try."

"To undermine everything Gram did?" I exclaimed. "To take us back fifty years and experience life in social prison all over again?"

He frowned. "You've spent too much time with Gram. Of course she has strong opinions about this."

"*Everyone* who lived through it has strong opinions about this!" I leaned over the desk, drawing as close to my brother as I dared. "Alex, listen to me. This isn't right. We can team up against the Firebrands and Virgil. We'll warn the people and send your guards to Neuromen to stop the update. But we have to do it now, or it'll be too late."

He pushed his chair back, putting distance between us once again, the expression on his face that of a stranger. Any closeness we'd once shared was overshadowed by his desire for the throne. He wouldn't join up with me, nor would he warn anyone. Because that would mean giving control back to Dad—and by extension, me. Alex would never give up the Copper Office now that he had it.

"Don't do this," I whispered. "The implant won't just affect citizens. It will hit Dad. Me. Maybe even you, when they're done with you. Think of Grandpa Vance. All the pain he was in, how miserable he was."

"You don't get it, Legacy. They'll do all of this anyway. *If* you or Dad does get sick, I've given the order to put you under until the threat is over. At least this way I can help you."

"Alex—"

"We're done here." He motioned to the guards. "Take her and the driver to my father's cell. They can have a nice little chat while we all wait for the update to drop."

TWENTY-SIX

LEGACY

DAD SAT on a cot in a five-meter-square cell in the basement. When Travers and I approached with our entourage of guards, he rose to his feet. It was then that I noticed his black eye.

"Dad," I said with a gasp as a guard opened the door. "Are you okay?"

"I am now. I've been so worried about you." The anger simmering inside me flared at his strained expression. Everything those Firebrands doled out to my father, Alex deserved ten times over.

The guards shoved us in. Travers immediately took his post by the door as they slammed it closed. By the way his eyes flitted about, I knew he was sending a message. I felt a twinge of guilt for not sending him back to Gram right away, but by the determination on his face, he would never have agreed to that anyway.

I embraced Dad but quickly let go when he flinched. "You *are* hurt."

"Those Firebrand guards have some strong feelings

about my reign," he muttered. "I'm glad to see you're all right."

"If you call being imprisoned all right. Dad, the update carries a disease. It's going to make a lot of people sick."

"I know. I've suspected for some time now, but I haven't been able to get the evidence to prove it. I considered asking you to help me after your Declaration, but I could never ask such a thing from you. The director has made it clear the lengths he's willing to go for this."

The words he didn't say rang in my ears. *We've already lost Mom. It would kill me to lose you too.*

The guards' footsteps disappeared down the hall. We were alone. I took a seat on the edge of the cot, allowing him the rest of the space. "We need to talk. Alex thinks I'm adopted."

He sighed. "Not telling you is one of my biggest regrets, Legacy. I'm sorry."

"Why didn't you?"

"Mom was insistent that you never discover your true lineage. She believed you'd think less of yourself if you knew."

I let the sarcasm frost my words. "Nah. Why would discovering that I'm actually a nobody matter?"

"You were always our daughter. Your blood never mattered to us."

"You lied to me my entire life, so you obviously knew it would matter to me and everyone else."

His lips thinned. "You're right. I should have told you when Mom wouldn't. She was always so stubborn about this. When I brought it up and she resisted . . ."

He'd given in. He always had. Mom won every argument simply because Dad stepped aside, letting her have her way and therefore her happiness. Once, he'd even offered to give her a work exemption that would allow her to stay home all day. I still remembered how loud their argument had grown that night.

The next day, Mom went to work as usual, and nobody ever brought the subject up again.

"You don't seem all that surprised," he said quietly. "Did you already know?"

"I have this memory of Gram and Mom talking about it once," I admitted. It felt like laying myself bare. "But I would have suspected anyway. Everyone else in the family is named after a precious stone. Gram, you, Alex. Just not me."

Dad didn't speak for a long time. When he finally did, he placed an arm around me and pulled me close. I rested my head against his shoulder like when I was a child.

"There *is* such a thing as a legacy stone," he whispered. "But you won't find it on any list. It's something your mom created at the lab before we were married." He held out his hand for inspection. His wedding ring still glinted from the third finger. I knew it well, having spent my formative years staring at it. The stone was clear, like a diamond. In certain lighting, it held all the colors of the rainbow.

I forced a sad smile. "You named me after a stone nobody else knew about."

"On the contrary. This stone was your mother's first real experiment, the one that made her a force in the science industry. She wanted to find a clear, unbreakable yet cheap alternative to glass. When she discovered how similar in appearance the legacy stone was to a diamond, people thought it might have high resale potential. But tests proved it too unstable."

"Unstable in what way?"

"Hit the stone with sufficient strength, and the atoms

violently collapsed to create an explosion. It usually happened within ten seconds of impact. Even the tiniest stones were dangerous. She didn't feel comfortable selling the technology, so the fad died quickly. But when we got engaged, Mom created two identical stones for our rings. We had them set by a skilled metalsmith to prevent an accident."

"Correction, then. You named me after an unknown, *dangerous* stone."

His eyes crinkled, the closest thing to a smile I would get tonight. "I'm doing a terrible job explaining this. Let me start over. When Alex's twin sister died at birth—the one our entire country expected an announcement on any moment—Mom took it hard. On her walk around the hospital wing, she found an abandoned newborn in the nursery, just hours old. She dragged me from the sofa where I slept and showed her to me, saying she was supposed to be ours. I resisted at first, but she was sure. So happy."

"Do you know anything about my birth parents?"

"Your birth mother signed the release in block text as Kadee Steer, but I wasn't able to find a woman by that name. It must have been fake. There was no father listed."

My shoulders slumped as I silently chided myself. She wouldn't have abandoned me at the hospital if she wanted to be found later. "It doesn't matter. Please go on."

His voice grew soft. "I named Alex. Mom wanted to name you, but nothing felt right. Finally, she announced she was naming you after her most precious project. Said her legacy stone was rare, beautiful, and carried a raw power that made it unique. Your mother must have seen all three in you."

I swallowed down the tightness in my throat. Rare. Beautiful. Raw power. It was poetic, but it wasn't me. At least the version of myself that sat here in this cell, waiting for a disaster I'd failed to prevent.

Dad removed his wedding ring and placed it in my hand. "My therapist says I should have taken this off by now. I don't know why I didn't, but it's yours now."

"Dad. Not your wedding ring."

"It means just as much to you as it does to me, and that's what matters. Besides, who knows whether we'll get out of here?"

"We will. I know it." I stuffed the ring into my pocket. Its weight was comforting.

It meant I was wanted.

"Dad," I began reluctantly. "The update Virgil is rolling out? I think it was Mom's. And I'm pretty sure he killed her for it."

He stiffened. "Go on."

I told him about the lab, the janitor, and Virgil's half-confession. I carefully avoided any mention of Kole. My cheeks flushed to think of him. Dad was silent through all of it, his gaze fixed on the floor.

Finally, he faced me, a heavy sadness in his eyes. "I should have discussed this with you before your Declaration. If I had, maybe you wouldn't be in danger right now. I'm sorry."

"So you do know something."

He nodded. "Virgil did steal your mom's experiment and this update was originally hers. But Legacy, he didn't kill your mom."

I stared at him. "What?"

He scowled at the floor again. "There's something Neuromen hasn't told the world. Brain implants aren't 100 percent safe. Studies have shown that cellular-degeneration rates increase around the implantation site. As a result, the person's life is shortened by a few months. It isn't much over a lifetime, but Mom thought anything was too much. Her intention was to create an implant that not only didn't hurt its host but actually improved the individual's health and extended their life. It provided bursts of electrical energy that renewed certain parts of the brain, kind of like a stimulating massage. A brain-centered Fountain of Youth."

I said nothing. I couldn't have spoken if I tried.

"It wasn't until a few years ago that she realized what she'd created. This update could indeed prevent brain degeneration in the long run—but sometimes it could also cause it to spiral out of control, the resulting disease incurable." He chuckled bitterly. "You know your mom. When she saw the potential of what she'd created, she tried to combat it. She refused to admit that her second project was as dangerous as the first. She wanted to save lives, not take them."

A heavy dread settled in my stomach.

Dad must have seen the rising horror in my expression because he took my hand and squeezed it. "Virgil demanded the project. She saw his intentions immediately and knew he would use it for the wrong purposes. One evening, she destroyed her research, data files, everything related to the update. She even broke into Neuromen's relay station and destroyed the backup files. Overnight, she became the only person who knew how to recreate the project. Virgil was furious. He ordered her to replicate it and hand it over to him, or her family members would start experiencing 'accidents.'"

The night she came home late. No wonder she'd looked so devastated.

"She wouldn't tell me what was wrong that night. I assumed her experiment had gone wrong again or something. I had no idea." The look on my father's face was that of a broken man.

My heart squeezed so painfully I wasn't sure I could endure it. I saw it all like it was happening right now—her expression as she entered my room for our nightly chat, her distracted state as she sat in her usual place on my bed. The pits of black around her red-rimmed eyes, her gaze fixed on the moon visible through the window. The unusual, awkward silence that filled the space between us.

Finally she stood and headed for the door before pausing to look back. Then came the question that had haunted me every day since.

"Which do you think is better—a life lived in chains or one lost for freedom?"

And that selfish, stubborn, *oblivious* version of myself had looked my suffering mother in the eye and said, "Lost for freedom. Nobody wants to be chained."

A sob escaped my throat now. If only I'd known then what the question really meant.

Dad rubbed my arm. "I know. I don't agree with what she did either. It's no use protecting your family when you also destroy them in the process. I believe she wasn't herself that day and made a poor choice. One she thought noble, but still a poor choice." He lifted his face to the sky, frustrated. "If only she'd told me. I would have confronted Virgil with an entire army. I would have made sure he never scared her again."

"Then he would have targeted you. But if she didn't tell you about all this, how did you find out?"

"She sent a delayed message. I received it minutes after the explosion, just before I received word about a fire at Neuromen. I hurried to the scene, but she was long gone. The message deleted itself within two hours, or it would have served as the evidence I've been needing. I think she believed he would carry through on his threat to us if I used it against him."

"But Virgil has the update now," I said. "He must have known enough about her research to recreate the project."

Dad looked angry. "He had files saved at his home, backups Mom didn't know about. It was a matter of months before he was experimenting on a duplicate."

"Then Mom's death did nothing but give him the glory and power he always wanted," I said bitterly.

Dad fell silent. Even Travers, who'd been watching the entire exchange, ducked his head.

We sat there as night fell and the cell went dark.

TWENTY-SEVEN

LEGACY

THE UPDATE WENT OUT two minutes early.

It was a vague observation in the back of my mind, like a knowledge that my heart was still beating. A tiny light blinked in the corner of my vision before the message arrived.

PLEASE WAIT. UPDATE COMMENCING.

If I'd been watching a broadcast, it would have been automatically paused. Any messages being sent right now would save as drafts. The entire IM-NET was frozen in place. I imagined Virgil bouncing on his toes with glee as the world held its breath.

Then it took effect.

I sat on the cot, slouched against the wall with Dad's blanket spread across my lap. He lay tucked in a fetal position, his head on the pillow, his mouth slightly open in sleep. There was no visible change. If Virgil had triggered it on the both of us, it could be a while before we felt its effects. But I'd expected *something*.

Travers sat on the floor against the bars, struggling to keep his eyes open. He didn't react to the update either.

"I should have asked this long before now," I whispered. "Do you have any family?"

He nodded. "A wife at home, no children. I've tried sending her a message, but it didn't go through."

They were onto him, then. That made him as likely to get triggered for the virus as any Hawking. Maybe his wife too. I imagined her at home, worrying about her husband's disappearance and trying to contact him without success. "I'm sorry I pulled you into this."

"It was only a matter of time. They'll have access to the estate's employment list." He gave a grim smile. "It's been a pleasure watching you grow up."

"No goodbyes. We don't know if any of us are infected yet."

"The question isn't if but when. It will be better for all of us if we can escape and get to a hospital before the symptoms hit. Perhaps they'll have something . . ." He trailed off. Travers knew as well as I did that hospitals would be no help against this. Patients were immediately put under to halt the disease's progression, but there was no cure yet.

I leaned against the wall again. Alex had made sure our guards were all Firebrands. Where were the guards who worked for Dad? Where was the military? Surely someone knew we were here. "They have to bring food and water eventually, right? We can jump the guards then."

Travers motioned to a variation in the bars next to him. A food hatch. They could keep us in here forever if they wanted. The only way any of us would escape this cell was on a stretcher and covered in a sheet.

"Do our guards know how long it takes to die of this disease?" I asked.

"No idea. Previous patients have lasted months, maybe years, in a medically induced coma. But this could be a stronger variation." He cocked his head, seeing my implication. "If one of us 'died,' the guards would be forced to remove the body. They won't leave a corpse here to rot."

"And that person could escape and free the others." The doubt hung heavy in my voice. The guards would be expecting a ploy like that, and I wasn't certain we could convincingly fake a death.

"The main characters did that in a book I read once," Travers said, trying to sound sure. "It could work."

"I strongly doubt it," a strong voice said from across the room.

My heart seized at the unexpected response. That voice.

A figure emerged from the hallway. He wore a guard uniform like the others and walked gingerly, as if injured. It was his battered face that caught my attention first. Bruises of every color decorated his cheeks and jaw, and both eyes were nearly swollen shut. If I hadn't heard him speak, I wouldn't know it was Kole at all.

"What happened?" I asked softly.

"My kind doesn't like deserters. Are you all okay?"

My heart gave a little thrill. He'd left the Firebrands to help us. To help *me*. "So far. How did you get down here?"

He grinned. It didn't have the same effect with his crooked jaw. "My kind are also lazy and tired. But we don't have much time. Our escape won't be easy."

"Do you have another stunner?" Travers asked.

Kole shook his head. "I was lucky to steal this one on the way down. We'll have to lift one or two more from a guard. Until then, my weapon protects Legacy first and foremost."

He strode to our cell door and swiped an object against it. It clicked, and the door swung open.

"I'll have it no other way." Travers climbed to his feet and stepped out.

"Dad," I whispered, shaking my father's shoulder. Then I frowned. The skin beneath his shirt was hot. Too hot. He only groaned. I rose and placed a hand against his forehead, then his cheek.

"We have a problem," I told the others, panic rising in my voice. "Dad's been hit hard already. He isn't responding."

Kole cursed. "I'll carry him on my shoulders. Legacy, you take the stunner." He slapped it into my hand and pointed to the switch. "Keep it on stun unless you want to kill someone. Aim for the chest or back, not the head. Easier target."

I nodded, letting my fingers curve around the ancient device. Modern stunners were light and small. Only enforcers, security, and soldiers were allowed to handle one. This weapon felt heavy and awkward. *This is the type of weapon Gram carried when she saved the country.*

It was time to finish what she'd started.

Kole grunted, my father's limp body slung over his wide shoulders. His eyes were pulled tight with pain. It wasn't just his face that hurt.

"Thank you," I told him, brushing my fingers along his arm. "I don't know why you switched sides, but I appreciate that you came."

"They took things in a direction I wasn't willing to go. But you're welcome. We have a long way to go yet." He nodded to the stunner in my hand. "You'll have to go first. Use corners and furniture to cover yourself, and don't expose any more than you have to."

"Got it."

Travers placed himself at my side. "I'll retrieve any stunners I can find and then take point. This time of night, there should be fewer guards than usual. We might have a chance."

"None of this chance nonsense. We're going to succeed," I said firmly. I stared at Travers until the doubt left his eyes and he nodded. Kole looked less certain. A sheen of sweat covered Dad's face now.

I leveled the stunner in front of me. "Let's go."

THE FIRST GROUP of guards we encountered was the largest. Thankfully, most lay sprawled across whatever chair or flat surface they could find, looking more like drunk teenagers than soldiers. They'd partied a little too hard after their victory. I stunned the only two who sat up when we arrived. Travers hurried to search their pockets, then shook his head. Neither had a stunner. Maybe the Firebrands didn't have the resources I'd assumed.

We made it to the main floor. Kole headed for the front doors, but I grabbed his elbow. "They'll be watching that exit. We need to get to the second floor."

He hesitated only a moment before following me into the lift. Travers hurried in just before the doors closed.

As I'd suspected, nobody was on the office floor this time of night. The hallways remained empty and brightly lit. No mandatory blackouts here.

"In there," I whispered, pushing open the last door. Alex clearly didn't miss his old office. Old bottles and a plate of rotting food sat on top of the desk. The office chair was missing a leg. There was no other furniture.

"Um," Kole said. "How is this supposed to help us?"

I hurried to the window and looked down. A large shadow was visible a few meters below. "There's a dumpster right below the window. Alex and I discovered the window was broken when we were younger. We used to come in and out this way to surprise Dad." I swallowed back the memory and shoved at the window, which slid open with little resistance.

"I hate dumpsters," Kole muttered.

"I'll go first." I handed Travers the stunner, sat on the frame, and swung out.

My stomach lurched as I hovered in the air. A second later, my feet hit the lid, and it gave way beneath my weight. As I'd hoped, the resistance of the thin plastic combined with the dumpster's contents was just enough to break my fall without making too much noise. I tried not to think about the stains I'd find on my trousers.

Travers followed and groaned at the smell. It took all three of us and a couple of precious minutes to lower Dad down safely. Kole landed soundlessly, wrinkling his nose, already looking around for danger.

Once we had Dad safely secured on Kole's shoulders again, Travers looked up at the window. "I did *not* believe that would work."

"It is impressive," Kole agreed, giving me a genuine smile. "Good call, Legacy."

I beamed before the reality of the situation hit once more. Gram was alone, and we couldn't contact her. Dad was in desperate need of treatment, Alex was a traitor, and the Firebrands would soon discover our absence. Not to mention that most of Dad's supporters most likely to help us could be among Virgil's targets. If they weren't sick yet, they would be before long.

"There will be time for celebrating later," I said. "Let's get Dad back to the cavern."

TWENTY-EIGHT
KOLE

Legacy's driver, Travers, stole a transport from a nearby parking lot. Minutes later we were speeding along the road toward the coast. After we'd exchanged what we knew about Virgil and Dane, Legacy fell silent, her dad's head in her lap. She stared out the window with a worried expression. The hospital was out of the question. The Firebrands would find them in minutes.

Since Legacy's communications were tracked and Travers had been compromised, I did a quick search for on-duty physicians and managed to convince one to help after his shift. Travers would meet him by the coast and bring him to the cavern later. It wasn't a perfect solution since we weren't sure who to trust, but definitely worth the risk. We couldn't just let Legacy's dad die.

We climbed into a hidden boat and navigated the choppy water toward a small bay. Legacy flinched every time we hit a wave, securing her father's head in her lap so it wouldn't flop around. It was hard to tell, but by the flush in his face, his fever was growing worse.

An old woman greeted us when we arrived. I knew her

immediately. This was the legendary Treena Hawking, the woman who'd defeated two armies at the Battle of NORA and led her people to safety halfway across a continent. She barely gave me a glance, her gaze settling on her son being carried between me and Travers.

"Malachite," she gasped and hurried over to clear the bed. We'd scarcely set him down before she waved us away and began covering him in blankets. I counted five of them. The emotion on her face made me feel like I was intruding on a very private moment.

Travers immediately left to fetch the physician. My shoulders and arms ached from carrying His Honor's unconscious body, and my ribs were on fire. There was nothing I wanted more than a moment of rest. But one look at Legacy's face as she stood in the corner with arms folded, and I made my way over. "I'm sorry about your Dad. Are you doing okay?"

To my surprise, she slipped immediately into my arms. Now that the danger of being recaptured was past, it looked like the full meaning of tonight's events had hit her. There was a weariness in her face that transcended a lack of sleep. "I'm not sure it's possible to be okay right now."

I put one hand on her back and stroked it back and forth. She'd described my feelings perfectly. "Nobody said you had to be."

She pulled back to study my face, having read something in my voice. "You didn't just defect. Something else happened, didn't it?"

I looked away.

She placed a hand on my cheek and softly turned my head so I was facing her again. "Tell me. Please." Her voice was gentle and pleading.

"My uncle didn't appreciate my helping you. He. . . took someone dear to me."

She looked as if I'd slapped her. "Kole. I—I don't know what to say. I'm so sorry."

I pulled her in again, barely noticing the pressure of her body against my sore ribs. She just felt right. "Sometimes there's nothing to say. I'm glad you and the driver haven't gotten sick."

She went rigid against my chest.

"What?" I asked as she pulled away.

"Fates," she exclaimed in wonder. "It's the blood."

"I don't follow."

"Our public blood and DNA records are taken at birth. Virgil said the system calibrates the virus to each individual. But my birth records belong to someone else." She grew more excited by the second. "Don't you see? That means the virus can't take hold. I'm immune."

I still didn't understand. "Someone else?"

She flushed. "I was adopted at birth. The real Hawking twin was stillborn. It must be her blood they recorded."

My mouth formed an O as I took it in. I'd given her such a hard time about her family, and she had no more Hawking blood in her than I did. "Is that why Virgil wanted everyone's blood taken again? To make sure?"

"Maybe." She bit her lip thoughtfully. "Gram said her spies reported a line of Firebrands at the hospital giving blood yesterday. But didn't Virgil make them an exception?"

I wasn't sick, so it had to be true. I refused to think about my uncle's promise of "something special," whatever that meant. "I bet Neuromen employees were spared too. He must have needed the blood samples to prevent the virus from taking effect."

"Mom's project involved healing people. That means it can be reversed. I'm sure of it. I need to get back into that lab."

My body ached with weariness at the very thought. "You want to break into Neuromen? You know that Virgil will have the lab under heavier security than the Block tonight, right?"

"I think Millian can help us. Will you send her a message?"

"I'll try. But Legacy, breaking in won't be as easy as you think."

"He'll be expecting soldiers. Enforcers. Military. Groups of people with weapons, not Legacy Hawking. He'll expect me to be sick, like Dad."

"Then I'm coming too. Virgil won't be expecting me either." Those guards had likely reported my escape already. They'd expect me to be halfway to Malrain by now. "Are you sure you can leave your dad and grandmother like this?"

"Don't be ridiculous," Treena snapped from the bedside across the room. "Of course she can."

We exchanged an amused look. Legacy ducked her head in a rare moment of embarrassment. "Gram, this is Kole Mason."

"I like you, Kole Mason, for the simple reason that you're helping us. This is where you assure me you'll take care of my granddaughter and help her accomplish this big, impossible mission without a scratch."

"I'll certainly try, Honored Madame Hawking."

"Oh, stop it with the honor stuff. Call me Treena. Does that stunner in your pocket work?"

I patted it. "Yep."

"Good. You'll need it. Now, you two get some rest before Travers returns with the physician. Something tells me you'll need that even more."

TWENTY-NINE
LEGACY

After Travers delivered the physician, he gave us a ride as far north up the coast as we dared. I snuck a peek at a few broadcasting stations and watched in horror at the scenes unfolding. The update was only a few hours old, yet the nation was already unraveling. Frantic people were lined up outside hospital doors, demanding treatment for their feverish loved ones. Storefronts were being broken into and essential items cleaned out. A group, faces covered, even broke into a pharmacy and stole every bottle on the shelves.

I knew what came next. Desperate people did desperate things.

Dismissing the broadcasts, I stared at the moon instead. It was past full, with a tiny sliver shaved off one side. In the choppy waves, its reflection looked broken. I liked that version even better. While daylight belonged to everyone else, night was mine. Sitting next to Kole with his arm around me, I somehow felt closer to Mom than ever.

She would approve of what I was about to do. I was certain of it. That fire inside me still burned bright, but it wasn't anger now. It was determination. I refused to leave that lab until the update was reversed.

When Kole and I got out of the boat, Travers tied it up and moved to follow. "Making sure you two get inside safely. I'm afraid to face your grandmother otherwise."

Hiking through the forest was even harder in the dark. My eyes drooped and my ankle throbbed, but I focused my thoughts on our mission. Fates willing, Virgil would be in bed now. We would slip in, reverse the update's effects, and escape before he even knew we were there.

"Millian just responded," Kole said as the white bridge came into sight. "Said she'll wait by the delivery station on the east side. Guess there's some kind of ramp there." He paused. "And then she said, 'watch that social anxiety.' What exactly does that mean?"

Grinning, I took his hand. "It means it's really her."

I knew the place the moment we arrived. I'd discovered it while wandering that first night before the blackout, when Kole had walked me back to my room. Situated by the kitchens, it also served as the location for trash pickup. I wrinkled my nose in the night air. Pickup was long overdue. I'd desperately need a shower before this night was done.

I turned to Travers. For the first time, I noticed a sheen of sweat on his face. He was positively swaying despite the still air. "Are you feeling all right?"

"Fine. Just tired." Even his voice sounded weak.

I placed my hand on his cheek and drew it back with a sharp intake of breath. Not Travers too.

Kole noted the worry on my face and pursed his lips. "Can you make it back to the boat by yourself, Travers?"

"Of course. I told you I'm fine."

A string of swear words entered my head, but I was too concerned to voice them. "Maybe you should get back to the cavern before you're unable to drive at all. The physician can help you."

"And leave you both stranded here? Not a chance. Now get in there before I have to do it myself." He winked at me. "I'll be waiting in the trees."

I felt my throat squeeze as I turned my back on him and headed for the ramp.

Kole jogged to catch up. "He really cares about you."

"It's mutual. Travers is more than my driver. He's my timekeeper and bodyguard, and he listens to me." I smiled sadly. "He was there for me when the rest of my family wasn't."

Kole gave my hand a squeeze. "Then let's be quick and make sure he's still with us when morning comes."

MILLIAN WAS RIGHT. A short climb up the ramp, followed by a crawl down a long dark garbage chute, and we were inside. By this time, my clothing was more old food than uniform.

My roommate covered her mouth and nose as we approached, her eyes laughing. "This won't do. They'll know you're coming six rooms away."

"Unless you know of some other clothes, you're stuck with us." I peered down the aisle of shelving, all in deep shadow.

"Oh! I know." Millian scampered away. A moment later, she returned with two kitchen uniforms. They were white and more easily seen in the dark, but at least they were clean.

I grinned and swiped the smaller one. "For a nerd, you're pretty smart."

"For a princess, you're pretty stubborn. Now put that on and let's get out of here. The entire building is on lockdown. Virgil ordered everyone to their rooms early. I've already scouted the route with the fewest cameras." She turned to give us privacy, gaze fixed resolutely on the door.

I changed quickly, all too aware of Kole doing the same right next to me. I tossed my food-covered clothing aside and pulled the uniform over my chilled skin. The blackness served as a cloak of privacy, but I snuck a peek at Kole anyway. In this light, I could barely make out the network of bruises on his chest. The outline of his hardened shoulders stole my breath. Those shoulders had carried my dad just a few hours before. Those shoulders had borne burdens he wouldn't discuss and responsibilities that weren't truly his.

Then his gaze locked on mine, and I was captured. A girl could fall right into those eyes.

"Can you guys stop staring at each other and come on already?" Millian muttered, still facing the door.

I slipped my shoes back on and followed her, fighting the deep warmth in my cheeks. Kole looked unaffected as he headed for the door, pulling the crisp white shirt over his head.

It was strange being here again. I felt like a year had passed rather than a single day. Tiny green lights illuminated our route in a long, straight line. Other than that, the hallways were as dark as they were bright during the day. I kept tugging my uniform down, hoping we looked like kitchen workers returning to the dorms.

We reached the locked wing sooner than I'd expected.

"I don't like this," Kole murmured, fingering his stunner. "Someone should have stopped us by now."

"I'm sure they're all behind that door, plotting the end

of the world." Millian turned and looked around. "My contact was supposed to wait here and get us in."

I stiffened. Kole groaned. "Let me guess. Zenye approached you and offered her services."

Millian's eyes widened in shock.

"That explains why they let us get this far," Kole said bitterly. "I bet she's turning us over to Virgil right now."

"Not true," Zenye's voice said in my mind.

Now it was my turn to groan. Virgil's internal speaker again. Millian practically leaped out of her shoes while Kole slid into fighting stance. They'd obviously heard it too.

Quick footsteps surrounded us, and figures appeared in the darkness. At least ten guards approached, each with a sleek stunner pointed at us. For the second time since I'd left Neuromen, there was nowhere to run. I lifted my hands in surrender. Millian scowled and did the same. For a second I thought Kole meant to fight them, but he finally lifted his arms. He flinched as a guard slid the stunner from his pocket.

We'd already lost.

"How long have you been working for Virgil?" Legacy asked the air, somehow looking calm. My every muscle was taut. I was ready to run, though we weren't likely to get far.

Zenye laughed disturbingly loud. "Longer than most people here, considering he's my dad and all."

The revelation felt like a smack upside the head. No wonder she had visitors and a private office. What an idiot I was. It should have occurred to me long before now. "You're a cheat, Zenye."

"Dear Kole. Wish I could say you look well."

"No thanks to you."

A slow laugh. "Just so we're clear, I didn't turn you in. You did that to yourselves. My father will send for you when he's ready. Thanks, Millian cutie, for the help."

Legacy's roommate growled as three guards separated her from us, leading her away. She sent a worried look over her shoulder before disappearing around a corner.

"Where are you taking her?" Legacy demanded, her voice wavering for the first time. Zenye didn't reply.

A hand yanked my shoulder backward and shoved me

back the way we'd come. I was grateful to see Legacy being pushed along next to me. At least they were keeping us together.

We reached a lift I'd missed before, all nine of us crowding in. I'd imagined some dark basement dungeon, but the lift took us upward. When the doors opened, the guards pushed us down a long hallway. I glanced inside the only one with an open door. An office. This was a section I'd never entered before. Legacy remained close by my side, tense as a cat ready to pounce.

They tossed us into the last room and slammed the door. A reinforced door, no windows. The only light came from the tiny crack beneath the door. There would be no grand escape this time.

"I don't suppose playing dead will work here either," Legacy muttered.

"Likely not." I didn't tell her the thought that lingered and refused to flee—that neither of us was likely to leave here unscathed. Virgil wouldn't appreciate the fact that his update hadn't worked on her, and I doubted I'd be leaving at all given Dane's creepy warning about my fate. Some kind of torturous execution?

I had a feeling Zenye was all too eager for the job.

Legacy plopped onto the ground, leaned against the wall, and sighed. "This didn't go according to plan."

"Don't blame Millian for trusting Zenye. She can be very persuasive."

Legacy turned a flat stare upon me. "Like that day in the garden."

I threw my hands up in surrender. "We don't have to discuss this every four hours. I have no interest in her whatsoever. If negative interest were a thing, that would definitely be the case here."

"I know. I'm just teasing. It helps to keep my mind off things."

Like the fact that her father lay dying and her driver wasn't far behind. "I get that."

"You mentioned losing someone. Who was it?"

I joined her on the floor. Cold seeped through the thin layer of tile. No wonder she'd wrapped her arms around herself.

Hesitating, I hooked my arm carefully around her and applied pressure. She moved closer and leaned her head against my chest. I had to force my muscles to relax and not tense up. Heat shot up and down every cell where she touched.

I finally spoke. "If I answer that question, you need to answer one in return."

"Mmm. Fair trade."

A deep breath. "It was my mom. But she was already sick. She contracted DNR-6 about three months ago."

She flinched, speaking in a tiny voice. "Your uncle killed her because you helped me?"

My throat felt like there was a stone lodged in it. It took a monumental effort to swallow. "It was my choice. You don't get to feel guilty about that." My decision was a burden I was doomed to carry the rest of my life, however long that may be. Mom may have approved, but that didn't lessen the pain.

"Yet you're here, helping me again. Why is that?" She pulled back to face me. "I don't understand. You were so . . . Firebrand before. You said the Rating system was inevitable."

I let myself relax, grateful for the change of subject. "Your grandmother reminds me a lot of you. I think she got us 80 percent of the way there, but that last 20 percent was a painful oversight." I softened the words with a smile I wasn't certain she could see. "I don't know if bringing back the Rating system would solve our problems, but something needs to change."

"What needs to change, in your opinion? I'd really like to know."

I thought of Mom working long hours into the night with no alternative. All the evenings I'd scrounged for dinner in empty cupboards. The mounting hospital bills that, assuming I got out of here alive, would loom over my head even with Mom gone. The run-down shacks lining the Shadows' darkened streets every night. Children who went to school hungry and returned famished.

"Someday I'll bring you home with me," I told her, "and you'll see the answer with your own eyes."

"I would love that." She sounded genuine. Surprisingly, I liked the idea too.

"Your turn," I said. "Your mom's accident seemed like an obsession there for a while. Why?"

She let my arm drop and pulled her knees in against her chest again. "Of course you'd ask that question."

"I can be direct too."

She was quiet for a long time. I fell silent as well, examining her while she gathered her thoughts. If you dropped her celebrity status, Legacy was still an uncommonly pretty girl. Her eyes were wide and intense, like a bonfire, and framed with long, dark lashes. Her hair hung long and thick, with a slight wave that made her seem effortless.

That was a good word for her, I decided. *Effortless.*

"I thought it was about my mom at first," Legacy admitted. "Everyone said such nasty things when she died. Called her stupid, declared women weren't fit to be heads of research at such a prestigious lab. Some woman-hater club even threatened Virgil, saying if he didn't reassign his women scientists, they would blow up his bridge just like she blew up the lab wing."

I blinked in surprise. "I didn't hear about any of this."

Her grin faded. "Yeah. Most people didn't. Mom was the smartest person I know. She didn't make big mistakes like that, and I wanted to prove it. I also convinced myself that finding evidence of murder would take away the dark spot on our family. I figured that would help Dad in the long run."

"You gave up an easy position at the Block to help your family. I think that's a noble decision." Far nobler than being forced to come by a bitter uncle. "Look, I'm sorry for all those accusations I made. I was pretty thoughtless. You didn't deserve that."

She played with a lock of hair cascading down her chest. "I didn't. But whatever one person says, more people are thinking. I've gotten used to people jumping to the worst possible conclusion."

"That doesn't excuse their behavior."

Legacy turned to look at me. *Really* look. It sent a jolt of wakefulness into my otherwise sleep-deprived brain. "It doesn't, but I can't say I'm entirely innocent myself. I said some pretty nasty things back to you."

I smiled at that. Every accusing word I'd flung at her, she'd shot right back at me. It was what first drew me to her. "True."

"But anyway, I convinced myself I was here for everyone else. My mom, Dad, even Alex. With me out of the way, Alex could focus on preparing for his future role. I didn't know his idea of the future was the *next week*."

I took her hand, curling it inside mine. "You couldn't have known."

"I should have. That tells you how broken my family is right now."

If her family was fractured, mine was shattered. It had always been that way. We'd never discussed anything that mattered when *both* my parents were alive.

A realization made me grind my teeth. My childhood was imperfect, but I couldn't blame the entirety of it on the Hawkings. A nicer house and better job for Mom would have been good, but it wouldn't have changed the things that truly mattered.

She placed her other hand on top of mine, her expression tender. "I keep bringing up my mom when your loss is so new. I'm sorry."

"No, it's good." My voice was strained, but I meant it. "I think it helps to talk about her."

"I'd love to hear more."

So I told Legacy about my earliest memories of her, how she'd been so carefree about life and head over heels for my father. Her rounded stomach one year as she excitedly told me her dreams about what we'd do when my brother arrived. Her broken sobs when the baby arrived early and stillborn. I still didn't know what they did with the little body. We couldn't afford the cremation fees back then any more than we could now.

Than *I* could now. Mom lay under a sheet at the hospital, waiting for me to make the arrangements, and I was stuck in an abandoned office waiting for Virgil to decide my fate. The hospital physicians wouldn't even know what had happened.

"I can see how much you love her," Legacy said softly. "I'm sure she saw it too."

"It wasn't enough to save her."

She pushed off the wall and crawled over to kneel right

in front of me, forcing me to look at her. "All the love in the world won't save those we love from harm, Kole. Love doesn't take away choices. It was never meant to."

I swallowed, unable to tear my eyes from hers. They were far more intense than a bonfire now. More like a sky-wide lightning storm connecting us in a sudden strike of heat.

I lifted a hesitant hand to her cheek. She accepted the touch, her eyes half closing. I stroked her cheek with one thumb, admiring how soft her skin felt. So perfect.

Then she was on my lap, both slender legs tucked to one side. She cupped my face in her hands, then brushed my hair back. "A Firebrand who loves," she muttered with a grin.

"No stranger than a Hawking who cares."

I wasn't sure who closed the distance first, but a second later, our lips touched. Her mouth grew more insistent, more persuasive with every second. Then her fingers tangled in my hair, my neck, my shirt collar. It made me crazy. I tried to remind myself where we were and what was happening downstairs, but it was a hazy memory when compared with this girl who was so beautifully, sharply real.

My lips finally slowed, hesitated, and drew away in painful reluctance. I could have kissed Legacy all day and into the night.

She groaned her displeasure.

"I know, but Virgil will send for you soon. He won't rest until he's cracked the mystery of Legacy Hawking."

"Mmm," she said, her lips still intoxicatingly close. "I like being a mystery."

I mentally grabbed hold of my brain and forced it to focus on something other than Legacy's mouth. "Okay. Let's look at the facts. Virgil won't come himself; he'll send guards. They may have stunners, but some of those guys were Firebrands. They won't have much training in weapons or hand-to-hand combat. Maybe we can jump them when the door opens."

"Two against seven?" Legacy asked doubtfully.

True. "I guess you could always challenge them to a race."

Footsteps sounded outside the door.

Legacy's smile fled as she rose to her feet. I followed.

A second later, the lock clicked and no less than twelve guards surrounded us, stunners aimed at my face. My eyes flicked from one guard to another, but taking down even one would mean getting myself stunned. Wherever they meant to take us, I had to remain conscious for Legacy's sake.

"Let's go," one of them said and pushed us both roughly toward the door.

THIRTY-ONE
LEGACY

Virgil sat behind the same ugly desk I remembered from last time. But the fire extinguisher was missing, and a giant board now covered the broken window. It gave me a giddy sense of satisfaction.

"Thanks for returning of your own accord," he said. "The Firebrand leader was frantic at your escape. Now that you've been recaptured, he can return to his bed in peace. I plan to retire shortly as well."

"Why wait?" I snapped. "You've already won. The update is out. People are falling ill. The Firebrands have seized control, and my stupid brother is in charge. There's nothing more you can possibly want."

"If there's one consistency about technology, it's that issues arise no matter how much testing you've conducted. You, Miss Hawking, are an issue."

"Because I'm not sick."

He cocked his head. "Indeed. I assume you know why that is."

I said nothing.

He waved a dismissive hand. "We'll worry about that

momentarily. I was just about to preview the broadcast your brother recorded last night. He ordered that it go out this morning. Care to join me?"

"I'd rather stare at a wall," I muttered, eyeing the creepy statue in the center of the room.

"Excellent. Guards, chairs for our guests. Then keep watch in the hallway. Don't let anyone come near my door, no matter who they are. Matheson, you may stay."

My guard—Matheson, I guessed—slammed me into the seat a little too hard. I grimaced, but the pain was nothing compared to the turmoil I felt inside. I knew exactly what Alex planned to announce, and I was powerless to stop it.

Virgil settled into the blue chair next to Kole. He gestured to the blank wall behind his desk, which I now saw was covered with a thin screen. It flashed on to reveal my brother's face. He looked tired but victorious, eyes slightly glazed. A script, then. I wondered whether he'd been the one to write this speech at all.

"This is Alexandrite Hawking, the oldest child of His Honorable Hawking. I'm saddened to inform you that a new strain of DNR-6 has infected many of our citizens overnight. Unfortunately, my father is one of them. It's with a deep solemnity and sorrow that I assume my father's responsibilities until he returns, if that joyous day ever comes. Until then, I'm determined to shoulder his burden as a valiant protector of my people."

His people. This was Alex's speech. I was sure of that now. Nobody else would say such a presumptuous thing to a country that was suffering. And this from a brother who avoided interacting with citizens as a general rule. Home tutors and servants were more his comfort level. It was one of the things that made us different. Was that why Dad chose me for his successor instead? Because I wanted to know more about those we led?

"In the meantime, if you experience strange symptoms starting with a fever and weakness, please make your way to a nearby hospital immediately. I've already asked all qualified medical personnel to report to work early this morning to accommodate you. While we won't know the extent of this illness for a while, I ask for your patience as we sort out the cause of this strange disease. I've also hired new enforcers to help keep the peace."

Firebrands. I was sure of it. I looked at Kole, who frowned.

"These measures will help, but I anticipate they still won't be enough. Thus I'm declaring an official state of emergency across the country. Continue your work schedules, report to the hospital if you feel sick, and send some healing thoughts skyward for my father. I know I'll be doing the same for you." Alex bowed his head, pretending to look emotional. Then the recording ended.

Virgil applauded. "Brilliant performance. Now for the other."

I stared at him. "The other?"

"The Firebrands' concession. This one arrived only minutes ago, set to broadcast shortly after your brother's announcement."

Kole cursed under his breath.

Sure enough, the screen lit up again to show a man with close-cropped graying hair and a chin that looked chiseled from stone. His eyes were even harder. This was a man who'd seen battle and was accustomed to victory.

Kole's uncle, the man who had just killed his mother. A chill shot down my arm.

"I'm Dane Mason, leader of the Firebrands, an activist

group that has fought for reform over the past decade. While our vision has clashed with that of His Honorable Hawking in the past, in light of recent events, we hope to find a middle ground beneficial to both parties. I hereby endorse Hawking's son, Alex, and pledge our hands to the cause of saving lives. We look forward to working with the new Honorable Hawking and are pleased to serve. Thank you."

The giant face winked out, replaced by blackness once more. Kole's gaze remained fixed on Virgil's desk, his face a blotchy red.

"Now, then." Virgil turned and hopped onto his desk, sitting to face us. "Let's settle the matter of your implant."

I raised my chin. "So you can make me sick like them? No, thanks."

"Being a scientist, it's critical that I understand what's happened."

"No, *I* want to understand. Explain to me what your purpose is here because, honestly, it looks a little crazy. You allied with the Firebrands and my brother and took over the government. So what? People will figure out that their loved ones got sick as a result of your update. They'll never trust you again."

"People tend to believe what they're told, but yes, I'm expecting the general public to come to that conclusion."

That wasn't what I'd expected. "Then *why?*"

"New NORA never cared about my career. Hawking has spent the last year slandering me to the point where people here won't look me in the eye. I'm no longer interested in proving myself to them. The rest of the world, however, has turned a very interested eye upon this little experiment. Now that it has succeeded, some very important doors will open for me."

I wanted to kick the man right between the eyes. "My country is not an experiment."

"All new countries are. I remember traveling here as a child with your grandmother, Miss Hawking. She was a lovely creature with big ideas, but none based on political experience or even fact. We would do better allied with a more powerful country. One that sees Neuromen for its vast potential."

I gaped at the man. Alex wanted to turn the country over to the Firebrands, but this was a hundred times worse. Dad had half his troops fighting in border skirmishes because of greedy outsiders trying to take over our lands. An underhanded alliance of this nature could be catastrophic to our entire military. "You're talking about Malrain, aren't you?"

"For a start. There will be others. It's like I told you, girl. The IM-NET has spread to every civilized country on the planet. Whoever controls implants controls the world."

"Until everyone stops getting implanted," Kole muttered.

"People are smarter than you think," I snapped. "They don't like putting their lives in someone else's hands. My grandmother's policies weren't perfect, but she gave up everything to create something better. And you just tossed it all into the ocean overnight."

Virgil smirked. "Then it was never that strong anyway. If I were you, I'd consider what all this means for my own country. With a teenager at its head, I doubt New NORA will last long as the fight over technology grows more intense." He turned to Kole. "Now for you. Your uncle has volunteered you as our first trial subject."

Kole's eyes went round and fixed on me. I must have

looked equally horrified because he swallowed. "But the update is already out."

"Neurotechnicians are always looking to the next project. This version is a huge step toward the future I've just described. Few lucky subjects will receive it, of course. Ethics and all. I would loop Miss Hawking in too, but her brother wants her alive a little longer. Just not conscious." By his tone of voice, he thought it all some kind of amusing game.

I tried to stand, only to be slammed back into my chair again by the guard. "Wait. What does this new version do?"

"Legacy," Kole said, looking a little pale. "It will be okay."

No, it wouldn't. My chest constricted more with each second, squeezing my lungs until I had to pant for air. These terrible men—Virgil, Dane. Even Alex. They had no right to play with us like this. If Alex were in front of me, I'd knock the sense back into him with a punch that would make my ex-boyfriend's head spin across town. I would give him the lecture of his life. I would set Dad's office aflame and see how he liked it.

Set his office aflame. That was it. Virgil was more paranoid about fire than anyone I'd ever met. Because of Mom's explosion? It *had* spread quickly, destroying half the lab wing within the hour.

I didn't want to put Millian and the others at risk, but with luck, a little fire could cause a distraction long enough to get me and Kole out.

"The experiment has been uploaded," Virgil said, his eyes distant. Communicating with his relay station, no doubt. "You should feel it any second."

He'd barely finished when Kole grunted.

I tried to rise again, only to be shoved down even harder this time.

Kole looked as if a thousand pounds had just descended upon his shoulders. His eyes widened, his veins bulged, and his face turned pink. He grunted again and slid off the chair, kneeling on the floor.

Virgil looked intensely interested. "So fast. Only eleven seconds in."

"You made your point. Release him now." My voice reeked of desperation, but I didn't care.

"There's no reversing this. Right now his brain is experiencing a series of massive shocks. I need to see how long it lasts before he loses consciousness. A little quiet would be nice, Miss Hawking. Twenty-two seconds."

I sent a desperate glance at Kole. He'd planted his hands on the ground and knelt on all fours now, ducking his head as if bowing. His shoulders shook. A tremor ran down my own body, my gaze riveted on his face as if I could lend him strength. He had already experienced the worst imaginable pain in losing his mom, not to mention the earlier beating he refused to discuss. He had only come to help me.

And now, I realized with a sob, he was going to die for it.

I glanced up at Virgil, who watched in fascination. He had to be wrong. Surely this could be reversed. If I could get to that relay station, I could stop this.

A strange weight pulled at my pocket. Somewhere in my anxious mind, it registered that the guards hadn't taken Dad's ring from me. The legacy stone it held was identical to Mom's. Or at least it had been, before the explosion. According to Fire Management, all that remained of Mom was a tiny charred and twisted piece of metal, barely recognizable as a ring, with its center stone missing. The legacy stone hadn't made it through the explosion.

Unless . . . it had *caused* the explosion.

Kole cried out, his face an unnatural purple.

"The disease is progressing much faster than anticipated," Virgil said to himself, eyes lit like a child watching fireworks. I snuck a glance at the guard standing over me. He watched Kole with a disturbed frown.

Slowly, I reached into my pocket and retrieved the ring. The stone was protected by a net-shaped cap. Keeping it in my lap so the guard wouldn't see, I grasped the cap tightly and yanked until the piece slipped loose. The legacy stone looked even more brilliant without its protective barrier.

I gave the ring one last, longing glance and let it roll softly down my trouser leg to the ground.

Thankfully, Kole's groaning was enough to cover the clang of its landing. I leaned forward ever so slightly, placed my foot on the ring, and kicked it gently toward Virgil's statue at the center of the room.

It settled half a yard from the statue's base. A bit too close, but it would have to do.

Another cry wrenched from Kole's lips, tearing free a piece of my soul. *Hold on.*

Then I bolted.

Matheson's hand grabbed for my shirt, but I twisted away from his grip and swiped the stunner from his back pocket as I danced out of reach. A squeeze of the trigger and the man collapsed midstride.

I scrambled for the statue.

"Guards!" Virgil snarled, but I had already rammed my shoulder into the ugly statue with my entire weight. Something popped inside the base. Another try, harder this time. Something cracked. I hoped it wasn't my shoulder.

The guards rushed over from the door. I managed one last kick at the statue before they grabbed my arms and dragged me away. The metal swayed.

Virgil's eyes narrowed.

The statue fell forward . . . and hit the ring almost dead-on.

A white light flashed beneath the statue.

I was in motion again. *Ten seconds.*

As the guards gaped, I slid over to Kole. He lay on his side, but he was still conscious. His chest rose and fell rapidly, eyes unfocused.

"Time to go," I said and placed his arm over my shoulder. Kole nearly collapsed as I fought to my knees, then struggled to stand under his weight. It was like lifting a transport. He grunted and tried to help, but it was clear that even one step was agony.

Five seconds.

Across the room, some of the guards now approached the fallen statue, staring in awe at the bright white being emitted from underneath. Even Virgil looked entranced.

I darted toward the door, half dragging, half supporting Kole. I kicked it open with my foot and launched us both into the hallway.

The door had barely closed when the explosion came.

THIRTY-TWO

LEGACY

I MOANED and pushed onto all fours, dazed. The world was silent, but it was an unnatural quiet that I didn't trust. My backside felt singed. I squinted through the misty gray fog surrounding me and saw Kole lying on the floor.

My brain snapped to alertness. *The explosion.* I turned to the door. Dark gray smoke slipped beneath the opening.

I'd done it.

I tried not to think about those guards inside as I scrambled over to Kole and lifted his arm over my shoulder just like before. This time, he just groaned.

"I'm not leaving you here," I told him, but my voice sounded muffled. He didn't stir.

I looked down the hall, wishing a gurney or something with wheels would appear. There was nothing but a series of closed doors. One that looked different than the rest stood to my left.

As I watched, the door slammed open, and a man sprinted out with a panicked expression. He didn't give us a glance as he gaped at Virgil's door, then ran the other direction. In the room beyond lay floor-to-ceiling equipment, consoles, and a couple of screen desks. This had to be Virgil's precious station.

An alarm sounded overhead. A few drips, and then the overhead sprinkler system came on. The equipment inside would soon be useless. If I was going to reverse the virus, it had to be now.

I caught the heavy door with my foot before it closed. Then, grunting, I grabbed Kole's shoe and dragged him toward the doorway. It took every ounce of strength I had left.

Finally we were both inside. I let the door close, rushed to the console and pulled up the public records database. There it was—every person in the country's blood and DNA information. I skimmed the options, not surprised to see there was no way to delete implant files. Of course they wouldn't make it that easy.

I found Kole's name and tapped the master control page. Scanning quickly, I felt frustration welling up inside. There was no reverse option or anything close to it. Every swear word I'd ever heard ran through my mind in a long string.

Fine. If I couldn't delete whatever they'd done to his brain, I would override it.

The screen glitched. My shoulders were soaked now. The water had to be affecting the equipment.

I pulled up Virgil, but his record was stripped of any helpful information. It wasn't surprising that he would protect himself. Had he done the same for his daughter?

Water dripped from my hair onto the screen. I swept it aside as I pulled up Zenye's name. Parts of her files were protected like Virgil's, but I could still access her implant version. It was different from any of the others I'd seen. No surveillance, no communication restrictions, and most importantly, a clean update. Perfect.

I stole the version number and let my fingers fly across the glass. One final keystroke and it was done. "Thank you, Zenye."

PLEASE WAIT. UPDATE COMMENCING.

Come on, come on.

Somewhere over the sound of sprinklers came a roaring noise. It took a second to register that the fire had reached the hallway. We were trapped. Worse, the wing could explode any minute.

For the third time in two days, I turned toward the window.

I picked up the heaviest freestanding object I could find, which happened to be a chair, and launched it at the window. My heart hung between beats, watching the black wheels beneath the chair spinning in midair. Then the glass shattered.

Two seconds, then a bounce and a splash.

A splash. The bay.

Peering out the window, I felt my stomach flop. This was no second-story drop with a dumpster below, nor was there a fire escape to aid our plight. Only a four-floor drop to a walkway between the building's foundation and a narrow railing that divided the sea. We'd need momentum and a trainload of luck to make that jump.

I grabbed Kole's leg and dragged him toward the broken window, wincing at the glass shards on the floor and thanking the fates for Virgil's glass obsession. Was the man even alive? Had he survived the explosion and managed to escape through his glass-less window? We'd have to escape to find out. The room had already begun to heat up, giving the wet air a swampy feel.

Now for the hard part. With his long legs, Kole could easily clear the walkway if he were conscious. But he wasn't. I couldn't carry him on my back or drag him out, much less run to get the momentum we needed. Mom would know a way.

An inch of water lay at my feet now. That would slow us down even more.

What would Gram do?

She'd once jumped out of a chopper wearing some kind of squirrel suit, but we didn't have that luxury. All we had was a bunch of heavy equipment.

My shirt clung to my body. That reinforced door could only hold off the flames for so long.

I hurried to the equipment lining the walls on the far end of the room and opened the lid to look inside. A second later, I looked at the lid again and retrieved a screwdriver from the top of the nearest glass desk.

It took several agonizing minutes to get the screws and bolts free, but the sheet of metal finally came off. It was flimsy, but it was all we had. A nervous flutter rose in my stomach, threatening to launch my most recent meal.

I shoved it toward the window, glass crunching underfoot and water sloshing into my shoes. Grabbing Kole's arm, I dragged him onto the metal. It floated a bit on the water. If it floated on water, it would float on air.

"Here goes," I muttered and threw all my weight into sending it out the window. At the last second, I threw myself over Kole.

We were airborne. My stomach felt disconnected from my body as we plummeted, weightless. Someone was screaming. A huge, hot burst of air whooshed in our direction. Another explosion? Whatever it was, it had just sent off my aim. Now, rather than avoiding the walkway below, I was trying not to overshoot the water.

I turned my body as the water approached. It wouldn't be enough.

With a mighty cry, I wrapped my arms around Kole and leaned forward. We slipped off the metal and spent half a second freefalling before hitting the water. The piece of metal hit the railing behind us with an angry metallic clang.

Kole, who had slapped the water like dead weight, now plunged deeper beneath the surface. I dove into the waves and wrapped my arms around him, yanking him to the surface. A moment's positioning and I held his back against my chest, kicking my legs to keep us both afloat. My arms already felt numb from the sudden cold.

It was only then that I looked up at the window we'd just leaped from. A strange glow shifted from its gaping mouth. The fire had broken past the door.

We'd made it just in time.

A familiar whirring sound made me want to cry with relief. Somehow, Travers knew we were here. The man had to have the sharpest eyes on the western coast.

But when the boat arrived, I couldn't believe it. It was Millian at the wheel, not Travers. He lay limp in the passenger seat, eyes barely open. My roommate halted the boat and began tugging at Kole's motionless form. I helped her haul him over the side and pulled myself in, suddenly shivering.

Millian pulled a blanket over Kole and handed me her jacket. "You need this more than I do."

"F-follow the c-coastline south," I told her through chattering teeth, accepting the jacket gratefully. "How in the fates did you find us?"

"The guards went running when we heard the explosion," she called over the wind, taking the wheel once more. "I evacuated with the others, but instead of meeting in the parking lot, I headed for the coast and found your driver. He isn't doing so well."

"I noticed." I turned to look back at the building. The entire wing was engulfed in flames now. We wouldn't have made it another minute. It registered as a dull fact in my shock-ridden brain. "Thank you."

"Thank me later. You Hawkings sure like theatrics, don't you? I mean, don't get me wrong—that was a pretty epic way of getting things done."

Two legacy stones, two identical explosions. Only Mom was gone and I was still here. Hopefully she approved, wherever she was.

"Did Virgil survive?" Millian shouted over her shoulder.

"I don't know."

We settled into a somber silence. Dawn was arriving, the rising sun shooting brilliant rays of gold across the horizon.

Only time would tell whether we'd made any difference tonight. Either the update had worked, or the country would be stuck with its current implant version for a very long time. It would take months to replace all that equipment.

Except Virgil probably had backups at his house. *If* he was still alive.

Disturbed by the thought, I took the seat above Kole and stroked his face. "You said it would be okay," I whispered. "I'm holding you to that."

A burning Neuromen grew smaller in the distance until it disappeared altogether.

THIRTY-THREE
LEGACY

"ANY NEWS?" Gram asked the physician as he left Dad's side. The man looked as if he hadn't slept since his visit yesterday with his stringy hair and unkempt clothing. The machine next to Dad's head ran on an electrical reserve since Gram had no generator here in the cavern, but it also required daily maintenance from a medical professional.

"Nothing." He collapsed into a chair with a sigh. "I wish I could tell you His Honor will recover, but there's been no change in brain activity whatsoever, no indication he'll recover if pulled out of the coma anytime soon. I fear that if we try . . ."

He didn't have to finish. Dad would die, no question. The disappointment hung heavy in my gut. The physician said my update had likely prevented others from falling ill, but there was little improvement in any of the sick. My hope that Dad would be an exception shriveled by the minute.

I'd plugged the leak, but I couldn't replace the water.

"How does it look out there?" I asked him softly.

"Not good. Hundreds of others are in limbo, same as

your father. Every cabinet member and some of their spouses. Most of the highest-class citizens. Only a small percentage come from the lower 50 percent income bracket, and those appear to be completely random."

Like Kole's mom. Chosen at random to lose the lottery.

Gram's face was an ashen gray. "Do they all remain in their homes?"

"We've gathered most to a smaller hospital in my own neighborhood to maximize the efficiency of my rounds—although I suspect there are more victims than we've discovered so far, so a single facility won't hold them much longer."

"We also need to increase security," I said. "The Firebrands might try something. Dane Mason has no love for any of those people."

"A good point." He looked up at Gram. "With your permission, Your Honorable Madame Hawking, I'll have the guard tripled."

I expected her to agree immediately, but instead, she stood there with one hand on her cane, still looking troubled, the cane trembling a bit under her weight.

I put an arm around her. "Gram, I'm sorry. We'll figure out how to save Dad very soon."

"It isn't that. I mean, that's part of it, but keeping him under will buy us time."

"Did I say something offensive, Your Honor?" the physician asked, rising to his feet. "If so, I apologize—"

Gram lifted a hand. "Don't. Please. I'm so tired of being apologized to. Thank you for your kind attention to my son and for raising an important question." She stroked my hair. "I've finished my watch at the helm. Malachite can't rule, and his son has proven incompetent. It's time we all acknowledged what my son knew all along. Legacy, it's your turn."

I felt the blood drain from my face. She couldn't be serious. "Gram, I haven't spent a day at the office. I know as much about politics as the sewer rats Dad had exterminated last year."

"Politics can be taught. What can't be taught is a loyal heart, and you have that. You've had it all along. It's why Malachite changed his creed."

"But . . ." My eyes darted between Gram and the surgeon, who both watched me with somber expressions. "The bloodline."

She knew exactly what I meant. "The word 'bloodline' appears nowhere in the ruling, Legacy. Not even 'blood.' Just members of my family, which you most certainly are. The fact that the country's leader chose you to succeed him —a move I happen to agree with—overrides any questions. If anyone struggles with the idea, send them my way, and I'll set them straight." She squeezed my arm. "Thankfully, you don't have to guide an entire nation of people through the desert to a new home. You just have to, you know, fix an epidemic, rip political power from a rival sibling, and overturn every bit of damage he's done. No problem at all."

I gave her a flat look, which made her chuckle. *I shouldn't have told her about Dad's decision.* Now I would never hear the end of it.

"I'm happy to make the announcement if it would be helpful, Your Honored Madame," the surgeon said.

"Thank you," I broke in, still feeling a little dazed. "But I'll do that myself. You have enough to worry about right now." How an announcement like that would work, I wasn't sure. I'd never declared myself the leader of a resistance movement before. I glanced at Gram, who watched me with a tiny smile, and felt a little better. She'd survived her experience by taking things one day at a time. I would do the same.

Kole lay on a makeshift cot across the room, his colorful bruises a stark contrast against his pale skin. The tattoo on his bare chest was clearly visible above the blanket. With his issue being different from the others, the physician didn't know the extent of the damage to his brain. At best, Kole would struggle to function as he had before.

At worst, he wouldn't wake at all.

I glanced toward the third cot, where Travers lay. My update had caught him before he'd fallen unconscious, which apparently put him in the best condition of the three. Millian had taken over boat duty for the time being.

"Tomorrow then, Your Honor?"

It took a second to realize he was addressing me. "Yes. Tomorrow. Please send me a report on that security increase." Now that Neuromen's relay center no longer intercepted or filtered messages, we could communicate with each other freely. For reasons unknown, Virgil hadn't targeted workers at any of the city's relay centers. Conveniently, most of them were loyal to Dad and, hopefully with time, us. I just wasn't sure how long that would last with Alex in charge.

"Of course, Your Honor." He gave a slight bow and left, leaving me reeling at the title. It made my skin crawl. That would take some getting used to.

Gram pulled me over to the soft chairs and motioned for me to sit. "While the men are dozing away, we need to discuss your plan."

This part came easily, as I'd thought about it all day. "First, we'll send teams to comb through Neuromen tomorrow. We need to salvage any equipment we can find and bring it into town. If there's a warehouse somewhere, that would be ideal. My friend Millian will take it from there."

The entire lab staff had made it out of the fire safely except for five—all guards standing around the blast itself. It was no surprise that Virgil and Zenye were both missing. I suspected Virgil was headed to Malrain right now with his storage of backup plans. We'd sent a rough contingent of soldiers after him, but there had been no word yet. If they failed, Malrain would be happy to accommodate a neurotech genius with the same hatred of New NORA they had. I doubted we'd seen the last of Director Virgil.

Zenye, on the other hand, was a mystery. Had she followed her father out of the country or joined up with Dane and the Firebrands?

The thought of Zenye and Dane plotting together made me tired.

"A million friends will take it from there?" Gram repeated, puzzled. "I don't understand."

I smiled. "Don't worry about it."

THIRTY-FOUR
KOLE

I SPENT entire lifetimes tumbling through a dark tunnel, chasing glimpses of light that slipped through my fingers. There was no present, just the past. Mom was alive and holding out her hand. Dad stood by her side, pre-Firebrand, and our simply-furnished apartment stood as if nothing had ever happened. There were glimpses of Mom's hospital room and a strange ceiling I'd never seen before.

The memories came fast, barely more than flashes of color. My childhood best friend's face. Bruises on a cousin's chest, the inside of a transport, an old pet dog who wasn't allowed in the house. Climbing onto an old rooftop at midnight to watch the moon during an eclipse.

There was a pressure on my hand. Someone nearby spoke, but the words slipped through my mind and refused to stay. I opened my hand to catch the words and the pressure increased. A squeeze. A gentle voice.

Opening my eyes required an impossible effort and several tries. The light sank away every time. I had to climb up through the tunnel to find it again. Finally the light burst in, exploding through every crevice and lighting my way for good.

I found myself in an unfamiliar room, though with the ceiling I'd seen before. Medical equipment stood to my left, old and temporary-looking. A window farther back glared brilliantly. It illuminated everything in an orange hue.

Someone squeezed my hand again. A shadow passed over my face, and Legacy came into view. "Welcome back."

I willed my mouth to cooperate, but my tongue felt like a useless, lumpy thing. She stood and stepped away for a moment, returning with a water packet. Soon a light trickle of water entered my mouth. I could barely catch it to swallow, but it felt incredibly good.

"It's okay," Legacy said, setting the water packet aside. "After what you just survived, talking may take some rehabilitation. I'll be here with you for all of it."

I looked past her at an open door. This was no hospital. In fact, it looked like someone's house.

"The cavern was temporary," Legacy said. "This is Millian's childhood home. They moved away several years ago when the owner willed it to her daughter upon her death. I guess the daughter didn't care for it because it's been empty for years. Don't worry, your uncle won't think to look here. We've been running operations out of it for almost a week."

A week.

Wisps of memory began to solidify into actual shapes as the events of the previous days took hold. Kissing Legacy. Seeing her brother Alex on a big screen. The pain in my head and a headlong escape down a long hallway.

It slammed into me like a transport. Fates. Mom really was dead.

"You look panicked," Legacy said, brushing a soft finger

along my scratchy chin. I desperately needed a shave. "There's a lot to catch you up on, but first, do you want to know what happened to your mom?"

I managed to incline my head. It hurt like Hades. *Don't do that again.*

She looked hesitant for a moment, though she continued to stroke my face. "I located her a few days ago. Your uncle sent her to the cremation clinic, but we intercepted her body. She's resting in a cold facility now, waiting for you. I couldn't let them . . ."

I managed to squeeze her hand back, knowing the pain in her eyes was reflected in my own. She knew how it felt to live without closure in her own mother's death. No body meant no cremation.

"Thank . . . you," I managed.

Legacy squealed. "I knew it! I *knew* you'd be okay. Let me go get Gram." She hopped out of the chair and ran out the door.

Her grandmother was here too? I guess Legacy *had* said something about operations. I took in my surroundings once more, but there was no indication this place was anything but a house.

Treena had almost as much life in her step as Legacy when they returned. The older woman bent over and stared at me, just inches from my face. She smelled of tooth powder and an odd combination of mint and vanilla. I blinked, startled at her sudden proximity.

"So you aren't going to die on us," she said, pulling back. "Good. We still need you. Although I think Legacy needs you more."

"For what?" I croaked.

"Legacy means to lead us to victory against her brother

and your foolish uncle. But she shouldn't have to do it alone, should she?"

Legacy, not her dad. The news was too much for my weary mind to process, but I licked my lips and tried again. "His Honor?"

Pain flashed through Legacy's face. "We don't know yet."

"I will always help." My voice was gravelly but firm. Whatever agreements her brother Alex had drafted with Neuromen and the Firebrands, I had no doubt he was in over his head. The crocodiles were circling, and he was too proud to see it. At least I could help Legacy navigate the pond.

Legacy nodded, her eyes warm. "I know. We'll do this together. But first, let's get you better."

THIRTY-FIVE

KOLE

NEARLY A WEEK LATER, I stood in front of a giant oven in a massive warehouse. They'd disguised the building's true purpose with columns and fancy pillars, but no ornateness could hide the acidic smell of smoke and burned human flesh.

On a gurney in front of me lay my mother.

I'd had a long time to prepare for this, but the sight of her still rocked me. Her pale skin looked almost a sickly gray, a plastic-like appearance to her face. Someone had arranged her hair in a side bun just below her ear. She would have hated it.

The cremation director seemed surprised that I'd showed up alone. I hadn't even told Legacy. Mom didn't have any family left, and I sure wasn't inviting Dane. Her life would end much as she'd lived it—just she and I, the two people who mattered most to each other.

I examined the cold, silent oven. The moment I left, she would be shoved inside. The director's expression when I explained I wouldn't be taking her remains home in an urn had been almost amusing.

He didn't understand. That body in there wasn't Mom, nor were her ashes. She existed only in my memories now. No vase could possibly change that.

Though out of a sense of obligation more than anything, I lowered my head and spoke a few words about how much I would miss her. Then I fell silent and let my heart say what my mouth couldn't.

I felt a hand grip my shoulder. I knew by its gentle touch that Legacy had found me.

Slipping my arm through hers, I pulled her close and rested my chin on her head. We stood quiet and somber for a long time.

"She's beautiful," Legacy said.

I nodded.

"My mom was too. Maybe they're getting to know each other wherever they are."

"I'm sure that's the case. Mom never bought into the Firebrands' mentality. She always admired your family." I didn't tell Legacy how Mom had disapproved of my choice to join, fearing I'd become like Dad.

If I hadn't met Legacy, what would I be doing now? Working under my uncle, sabotaging the government, and hurting the Hawkings any way I could? Or would I eventually have seen what Mom had intended for me all along?

"I thought you went to a meeting with Millian," I said. Legacy's roommate had taken initiative over Legacy's makeshift neurotech unit in a warehouse across town. Nearly two entire Neuromen wings had burned down, but they'd salvaged about a quarter of the equipment. If nothing else, they'd be keeping it from Virgil. Wherever he was.

"Millian wants to disable the implants," Legacy said, her voice low so we wouldn't be overheard. The funeral director was nowhere to be seen now, but I suspected he was nearby, waiting for us to leave. "But the physicians say our brains have evolved to rely on them at this point. Removing them could make things far worse."

"What about Malrain?" I asked. If the Firebrands were crocodiles circling an injured animal, our neighboring country was a group of vultures ready to pounce. I wasn't sure which would take us first.

It was remarkable how the country had changed in just eight days. Food was scarce, and the people were distrustful and hardened and fought to secure protection for their families. Employment was hit-and-miss. National transportation was down.

I'd helped to make that happen. Now I would work to unravel it and create something better.

I took Legacy's hand. "I'm ready. Let's go."

"You said your goodbyes?"

I smiled tightly at my mother. "I said them before she passed." They just hadn't been verbal.

Legacy wrapped me in an embrace. "Let's make sure we don't have to say any more goodbyes for a while." I knew she was thinking of her father and brother. One recovered in a makeshift hospital room across town, separate from where we stayed but closer to medical help. The other sat in a stolen office made of copper, ignoring how the country crumbled under his hand.

Something told me the goodbyes weren't finished yet, but I didn't tell her so. I simply squeezed her hand as we left the crematory and emerged into the wider world.

LEGACY AND KOLE'S STORY CONTINUES
in the series finale, *Numbers Collide, available now!*

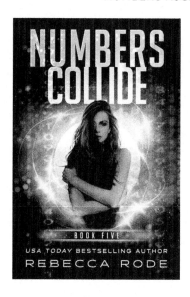

BEFORE YOU GO...

GET FOUR FREE CHARACTER STORIES when you join Rebecca's Readers! You'll also get exclusive pricing, access to early releases, and free bonus content. You can unsubscribe anytime, no hard feelings whatsoever. Visit www. AuthorRebeccaRode.com to join.

LOVE FANTASY & PIRATES?

Decades ago, a band of female pirates nearly conquered the world. Now the king executes female sailors—which complicates Laney's dream of becoming captain. She must disguise herself as a boy in order to survive.

But when the king's son asks Laney to help him save his father's kingdom, Laney must embrace the danger of discovery for the possibility for the life she's always wanted.

It's time to pull off a mutiny of her own.

NOW AVAILABLE AT ALL MAJOR RETAILERS

EXPERIENCE A NEW KIND OF DYSTOPIAN

Ember knows three things for certain.

- She sees the future.
- They want to turn her into the galaxy's deadliest weapon.
- Even the strongest weapons can backfire.

If you love epic space sagas, experience Flicker now!

ABOUT THE AUTHOR

REBECCA RODE is a *USA Today* and *Wall Street Journal* bestselling author. Her published fiction includes the Numbers Game Saga, the Ember in Space trilogy, and TIDES OF MUTINY (Little, Brown Young Readers). She has also published nonfiction and online news articles for several publications, but she prefers writing for teens and the young at heart. She is represented by Kelly Peterson at Rees Literary. Visit Rebecca at AuthorRebeccaRode.com.

Printed in Great Britain
by Amazon